The Roadkill of Middle Earth

A PARODY BY
John Carnell

ILLUSTRATED BY
Tom Sutton

D1417444

ibooks
new
www.ibooksinc.com

DISTRIBUTED BY SIMON & SCHUSTER, INC.

An Original Publication of ibooks, inc.

Copyright © 2001 ibooks, inc.

Cover art by Rich Larson and Steve Fastner
Cover and interior design by Mike Rivilis

An ibooks, inc. Book

Distributed by Simon & Schuster, Inc.
1230 Avenue of the Americas, New York, NY 10020

ibooks, inc.
24 West 25th Street
New York, NY
10010
www.ibooksinc.com

ISBN 0-7434-3467-6

First ibooks, inc. printing October 2001
10 9 8 7 6 5 4 3 2 1

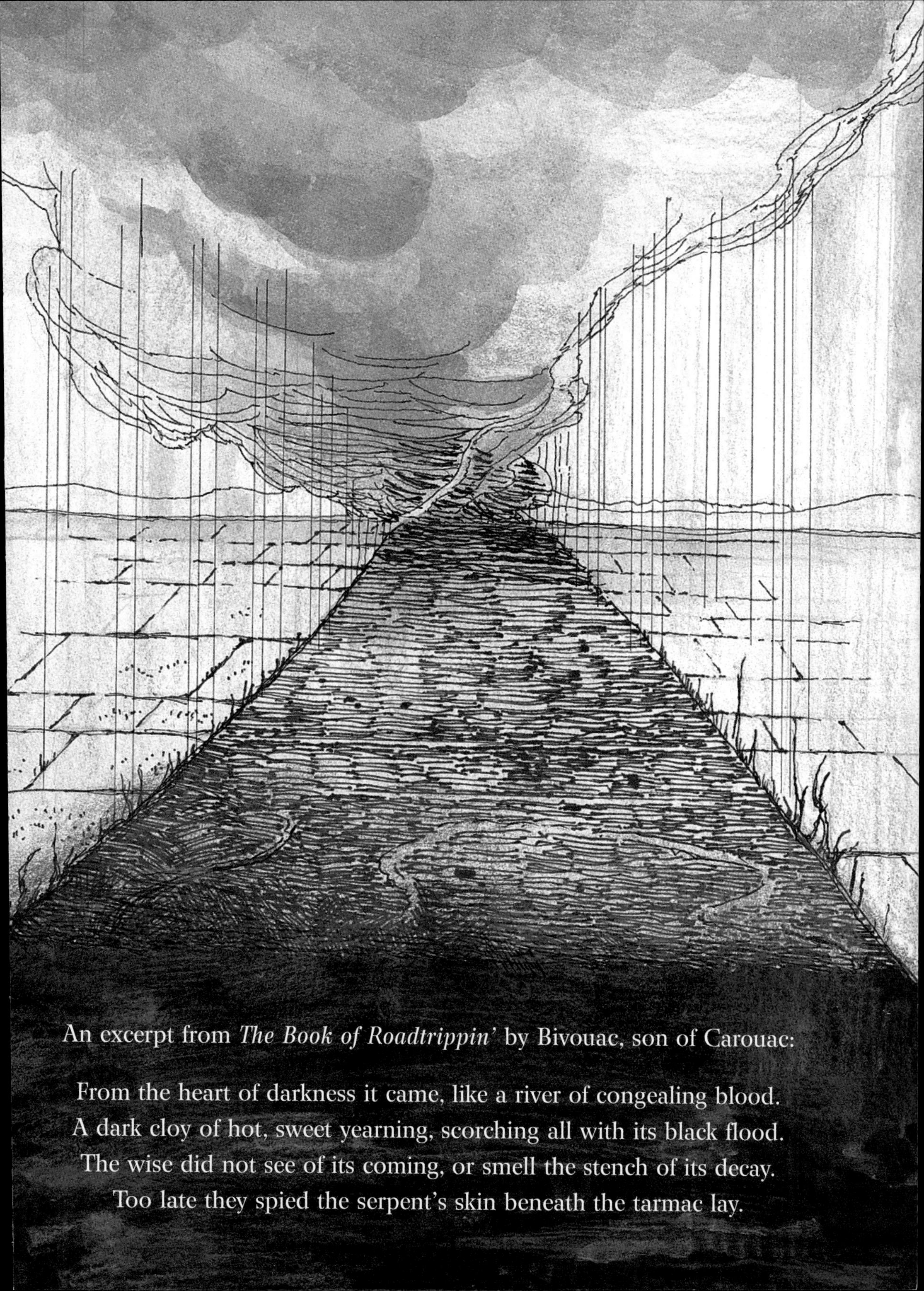

An excerpt from *The Book of Roadtrippin'* by Bivouac, son of Carouac:

From the heart of darkness it came, like a river of congealing blood.
A dark cloy of hot, sweet yearning, scorching all with its black flood.
The wise did not see of its coming, or smell the stench of its decay.
Too late they spied the serpent's skin beneath the tarmac lay.

It came from the South. Some called it the RHYDDE. Others, less well versed in the Elven tongue, called it THE ROAD.*

*Of course, much verse chronicled the days of its coming and some can still be found in the Highway Ode, but as most of it is way too tedious, that's a trip we won't be taking—although it may well be worth showing you, gentle readers, an extract from the aforementioned book so you'll understand why:

> "Abridge, abreast, it headed west , through field and
> wood did clamber.
> Alas, Aghast, a pace so fast, that none could bear its
> camber.
> Up Hill and Vale and down the Dale, its race was
> unrelenting.
> 'til work was done, and it had won, the rhydde, our
> death cementing."
>
> (from "The Song of the Black Death"
> by Winnebago Morrisett)

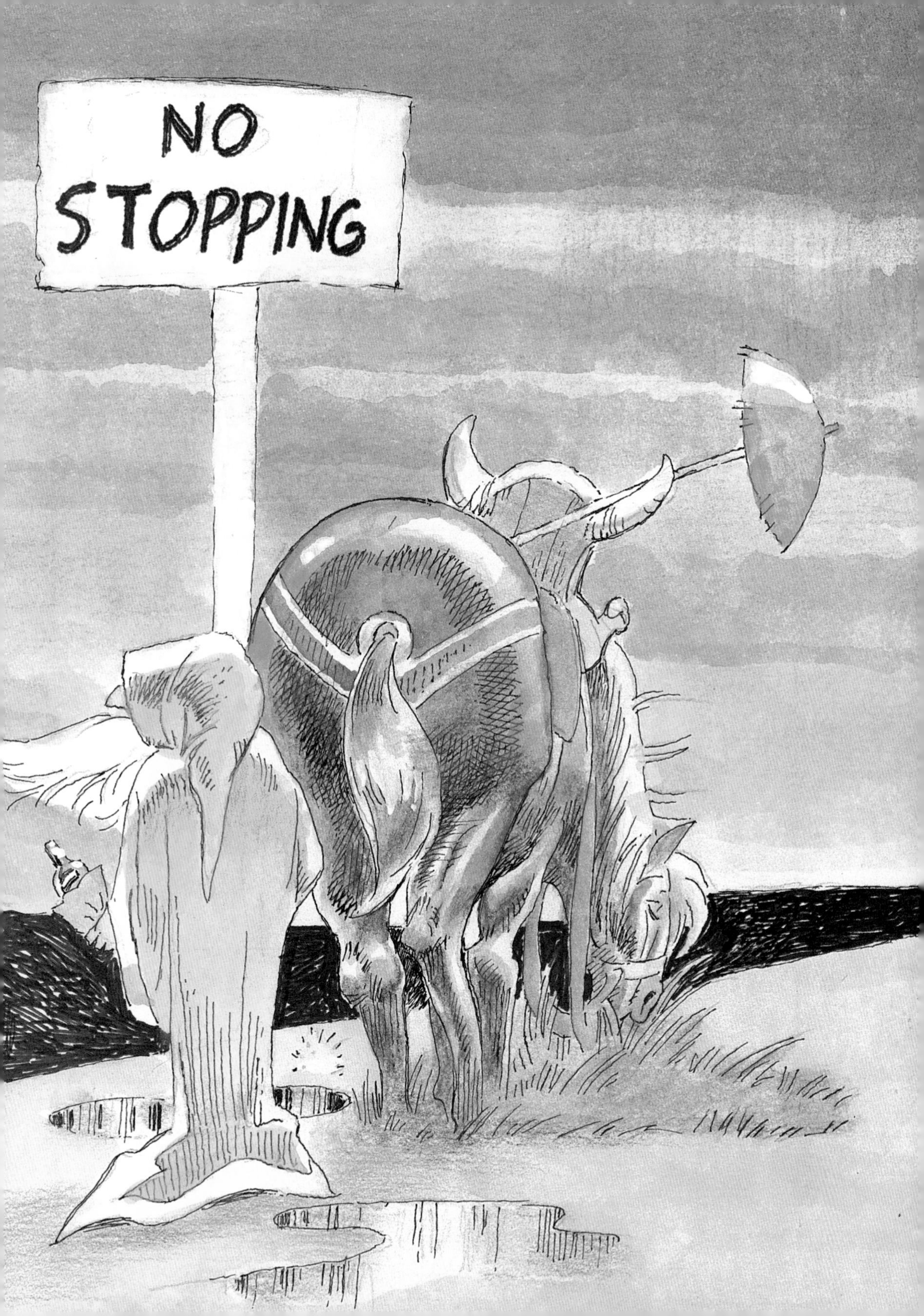
NO
STOPPING

ome said the Road came from a dark continent across the Baffling Bay. Others, a land so dread that none shall speak its name but in a hushed whisper . . . but I'll give you a clue . . . MORDOUR!* Only the very wise and the very foolish dared travel the black highway through Middle Terra Firma. For it was said that along this highway a mighty Dragon called Smog plied its awful trade.

*Mordour: The heart of darkness. A filth-encrusted quagmire of evil stench. A doom-laden lair of unimaginable horror. A rank vista, home to a festering purulence. Zit central. The pits. As bad as a bachelor's bedroom after a three-day weekend.

(from *The Pocket Guide to Mordour and Other Suicidal Hotspots*)

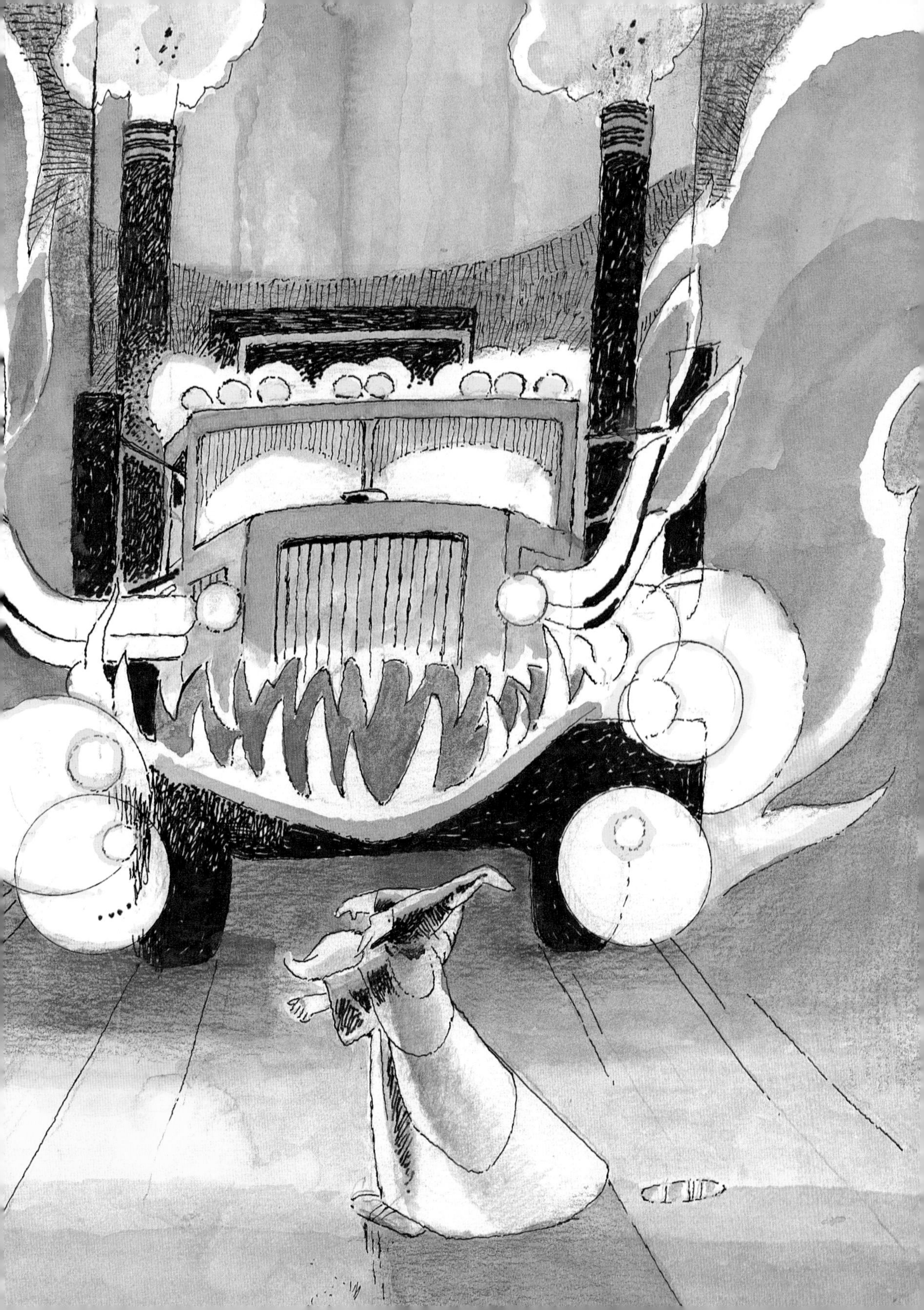

In these days of great consternation the gap between the very wise and the very foolish was now almost closed. Randolf Shortshanks, the Wizard, had long since swapped sorcery for saucery* and met Smog on the way back from the liquor store. It was a brief and sordid encounter in which Smog hit the bottle, but Shortshanks was the one who got smashed!

*Saucery: A widely abused form of magic often engaged in by old wizards who have fallen by the wayside. Under a typical saucery spell the practitioner is able to cause his or her head to spin in unnatural ways, walk like a three-legged moose and projectile vomit multicolored roons** onto pavements.

**Roons: small bits of mystic pizza, so-called because of their onomatopoeic nature.

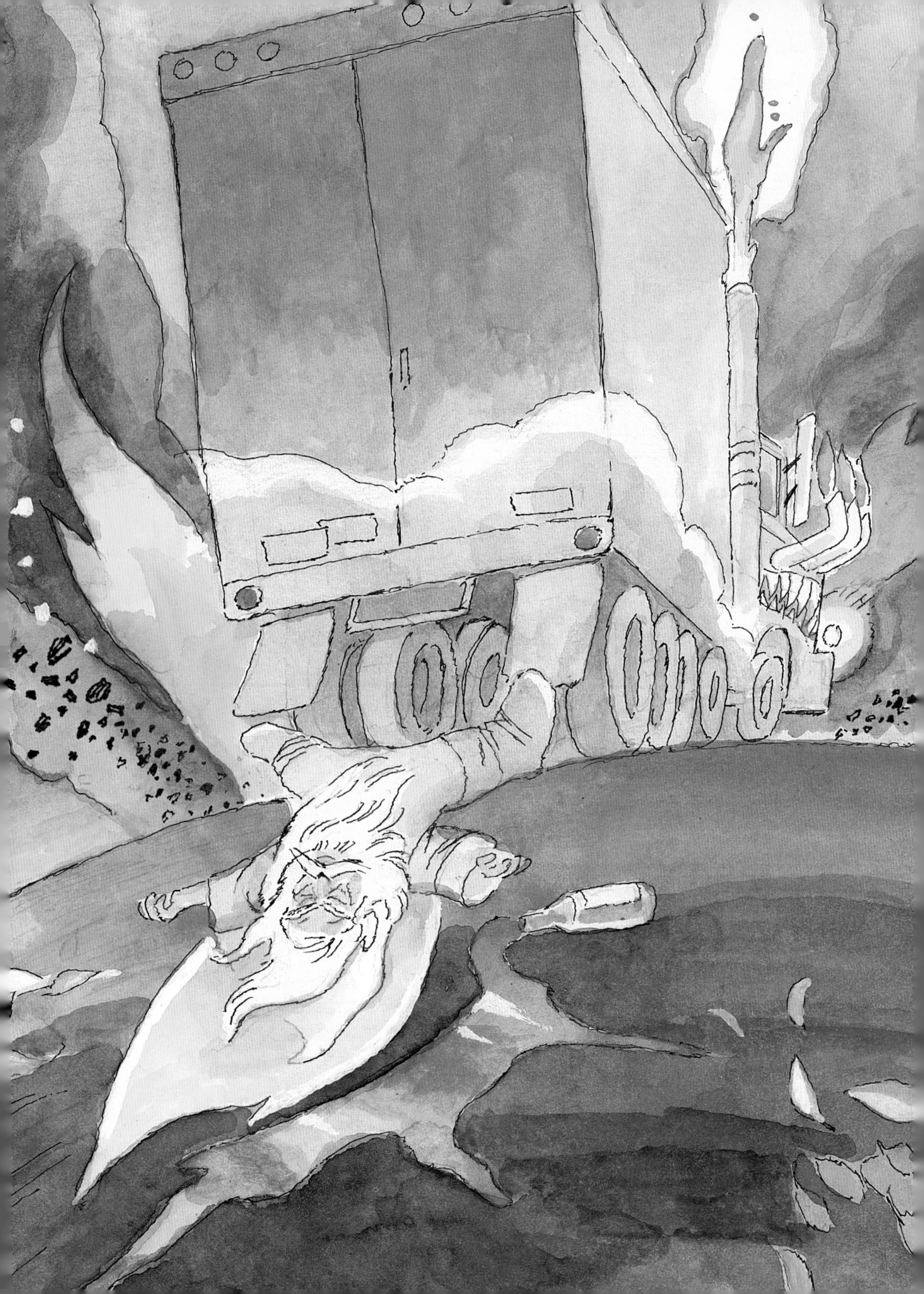

mog, it seemed, was restless, without home. The mighty dragon liked nothing better than wandering the highways and byways of Middle Terra Firma, clocking up roadkill.* The once idyllic meadows and pastures were resown by his awesome tyres. Elves and other lithesome Fairyfolk were ploughed under as Smog went off the road.

*Roadkill: This is of course a Dragon's favourite pastime and also later to be the name of a best-selling board game. The object of the game is for each player to outscore his opponents by squashing as many Elves, Pixies and Fairyfolk as possible with their choice of truck while racing from Mordour to the Shyer. Plus points are given for "hitting" bands of Little People and Mythical Warriors, and top points can be earned for flattening Drunken Wizards with no road sense. "Bad Driving" trump cards award the player with extra points on their license. These protect against Highway Pay-trolls who can pull you over and make you miss a turn for such offences as "view through windshield unimpeded by blood," "failing to display severed body parts on grill," and "not driving while under the influence of mind-bending drugs."

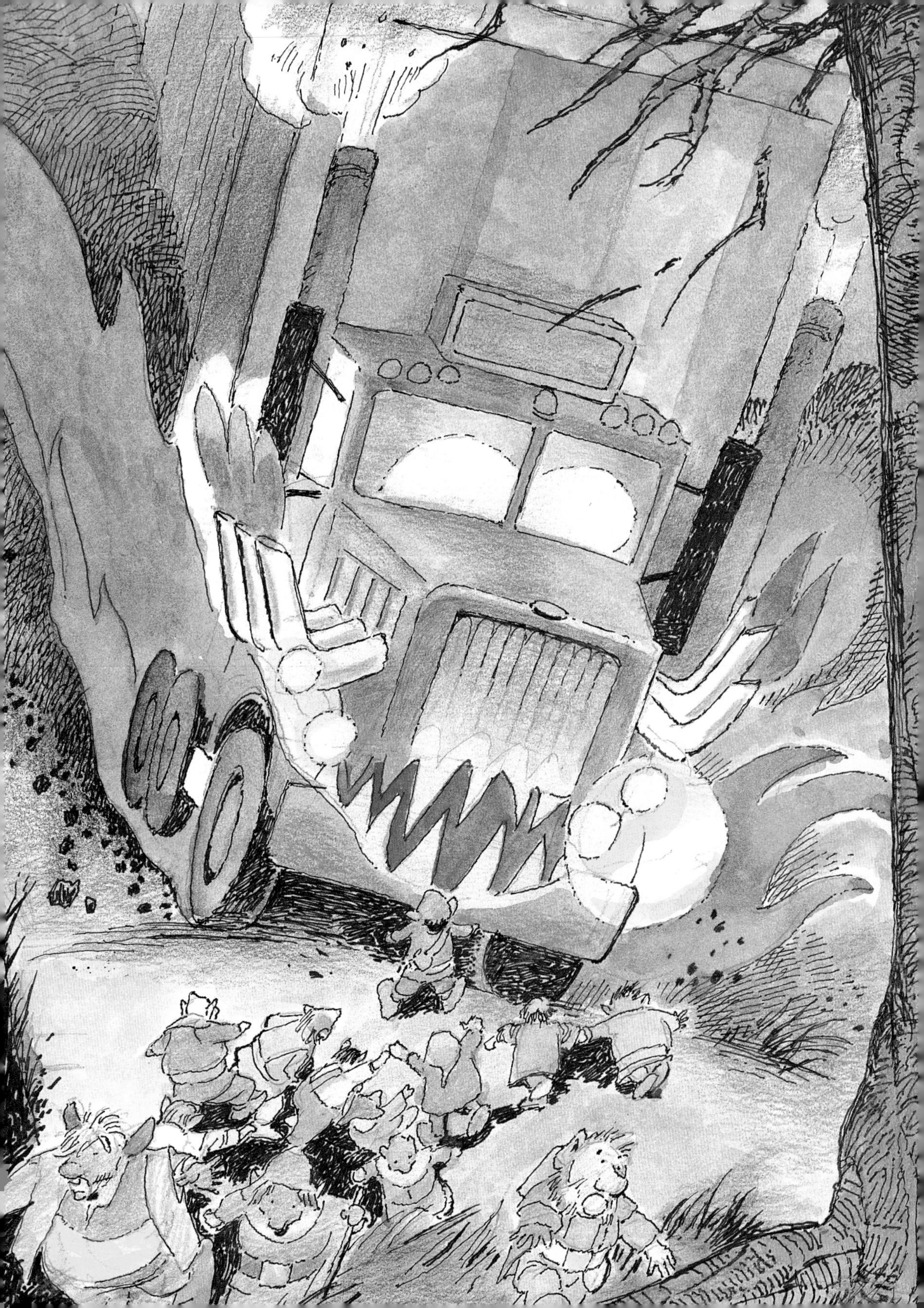

mog showed his victims no mercy. His fiery heart roared as he hit and ran. The only tears he shed, were of acid concentrate, burning his windshield clean of Elfin entrails.* But Smog himself was in the grip of a much greater terror, the one they simply called The Dark Rider.

*Miss a turn. Acid concentrate is strictly prohibited for anything other than dissolving Fairyfolk sucked up in the turbo-charger.

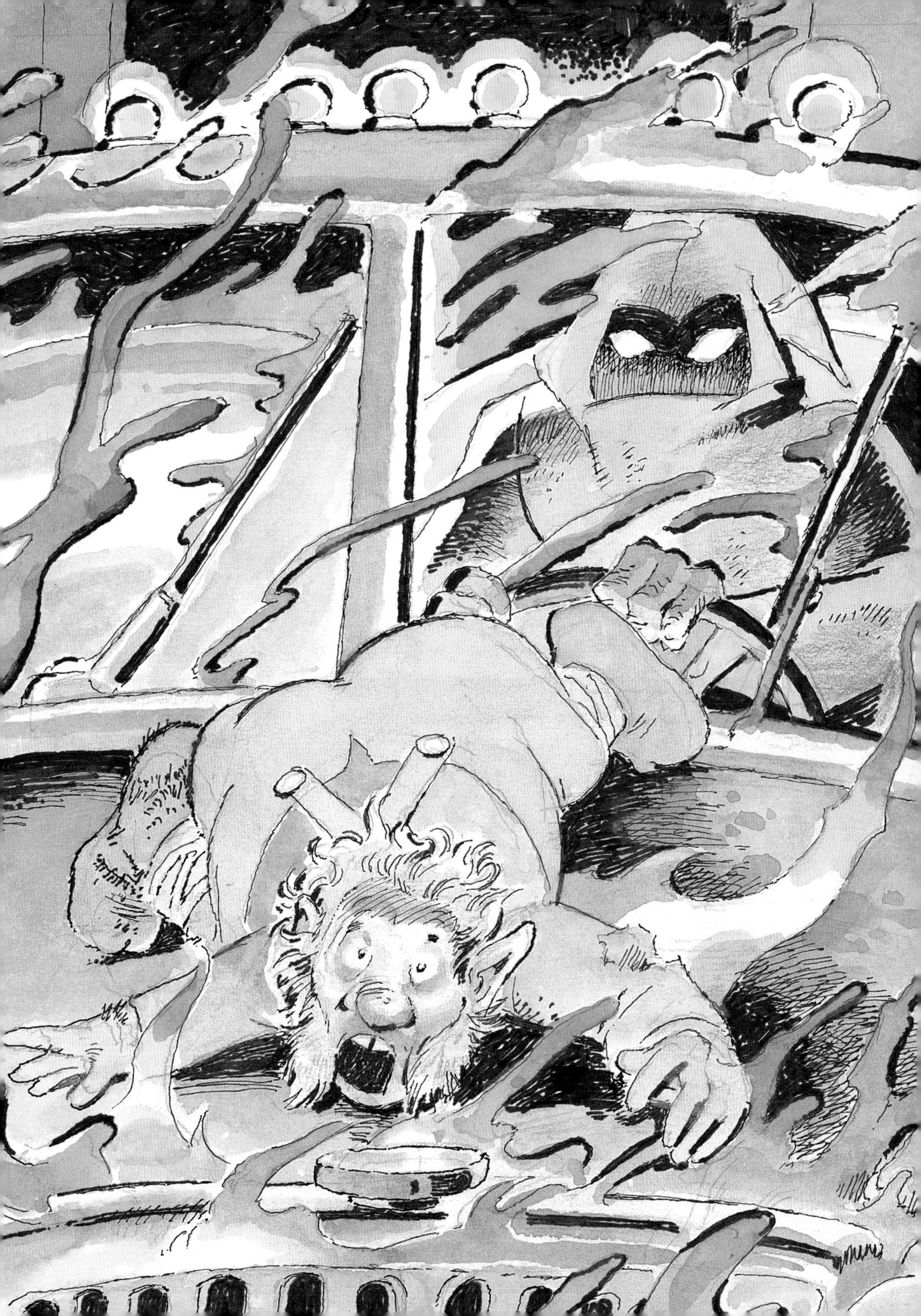

I t was he, The Dark Rider, who was in the driver's seat, and had his wicked hands clasped firmly on the wheel. Where he came from and where he was going nobody knew, but one thing was for sure . . . there was no mistaking where he had been.*

*If they had bought the board game, they'd have know full well that The Dark Rider hailed from Mordour. Then of course, they could have avoided a messy, gratuitous end. Hindsight—such a wonderful thing. The rearview mirror of life.

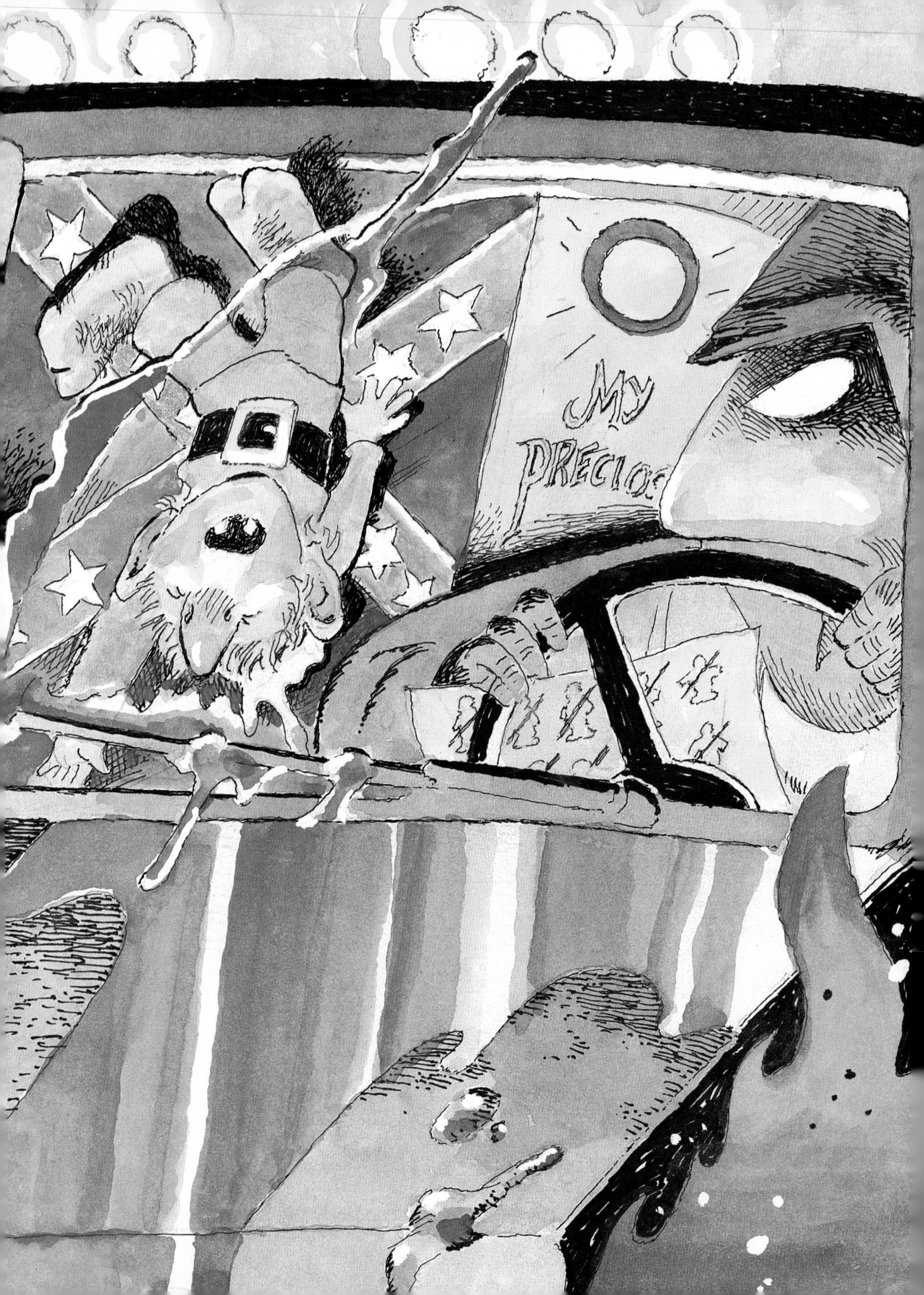
My
PRECIOS

one could outrun The Dark Rider. Not even the famed Horsemen of Roham.* Their steeds were as donkeys before his impressive horsepower. Their once matchless equine specimens were ridden into the dirt and their riders lost like bank notes in a bookmaker's satchel. Tossed away, never to be seen again. In this race there was only one certainty—a future as roadkill.

*The famed Horsemen of Roham were famed for the fact that their horses were the finest steeds ever to set hoof on Middle Terra Firma, but also widely admired for their ability to whisper** a horse.

**Whisper: Whispering is the ancient art of blowing a horse—an illegal act in some parts of Terra Firma, but celebrated by the inhabitants of Roham, whose gentle and persuasive breathing into the horses nostril is said to give the rider an empathetic bond with his mount.

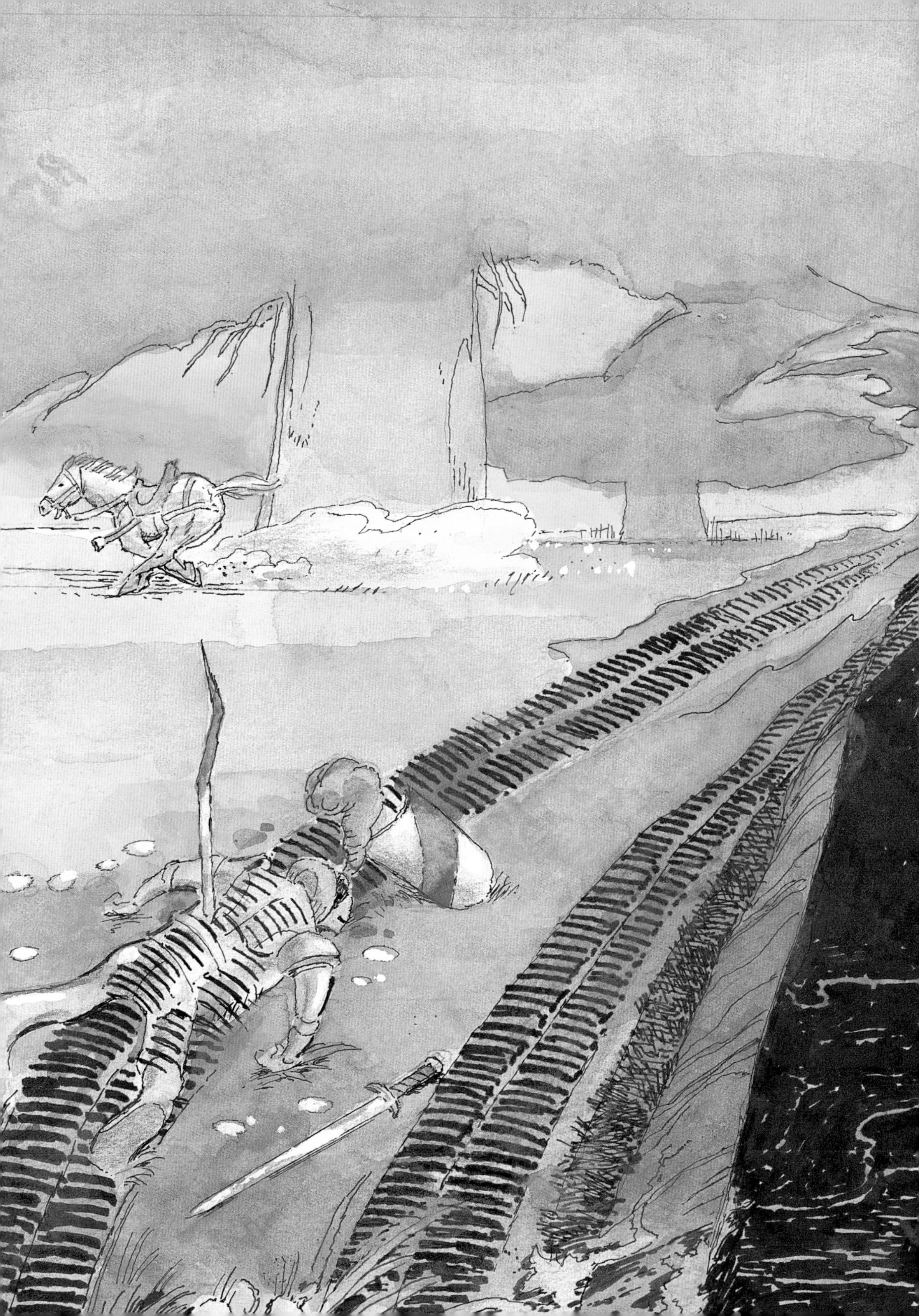

he tired and the careless were always easy pickings. A sad end to a hard day's graft under the dark mountains. No more will this Dwarf hi-ho his way home to a warmly lit hovel, and smoke homegrown weeds with his wife. He has chipped his last block, dug his final hole, and will soon be six foot under. Chiseled on his tombstone should be the inscription: Here lies the bones of Ownwin Groaning, crossing the road, the road crossed Ownwin.*

*The inscriptions on Dwarfish tombstones are often witty and tell of a living fondness for humour among a people often portrayed as gruff and grouchy (not to mention the other five!). At Dwarf funerals it is considered good etiquette to dance on the graves of the freshly dead whilst reciting a short ditty mocking their weak points. You can find some of the better ones captured forever in the short tome entitled *Requiem for the Missus*, compiled by Hoaning, husband to Moaning-and-Groaning, son of Phoaning. (Published by Dodder and Slaughter.)

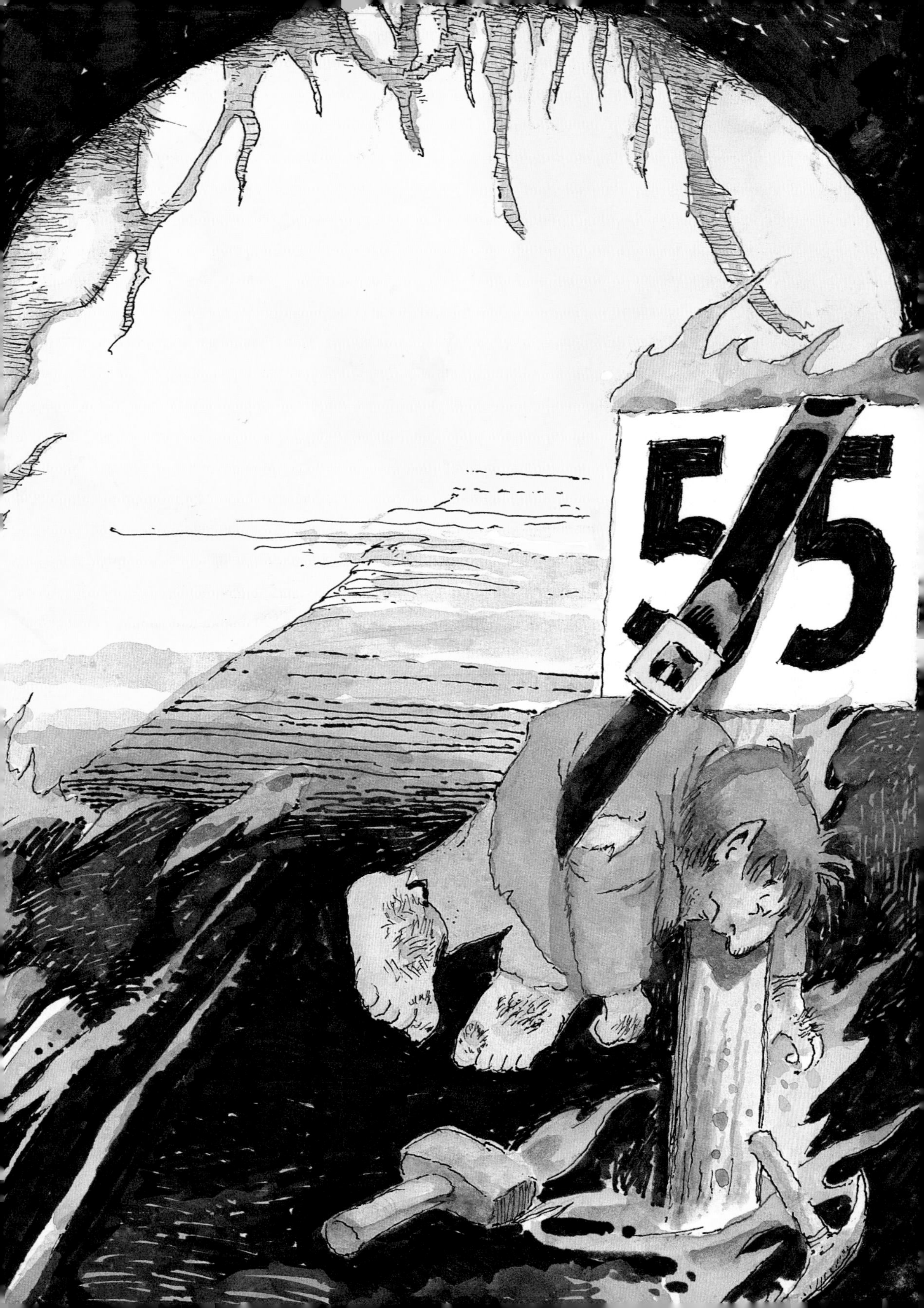
5 5

ven the road-wise, those most skilled in tracking, could not escape. More pity this noble tracker* didn't see his destiny bearing down on him round the hairpin. At least his life is not wasted on those who would come behind. There could be no misreading of these tracks!

*Tracker: Terra Firma's equivalent to a Slacker. A work-shy fop, usually related to aristocracy, who loafs about from one village to the next pretending to divine the future from the convergence of cracks in the road. In exchange for fare provided by gullible villagers, trackers will often cobble together a sort of horoscope depending on the person's road sign. These are highly fanciful and tend to depend on what sign is on the incline. An example: "Maximum speed 50" in conjunction with a rising "Dead End " sign, could be interpreted as *trouble lies ahead*. "No Parking" in the house of Elrond could signal a journey, and "Stop! Troll Bridge Ahead" is *always* read as a bad omen. (For more information, see the back of the afore-mentioned Highway Ode.)

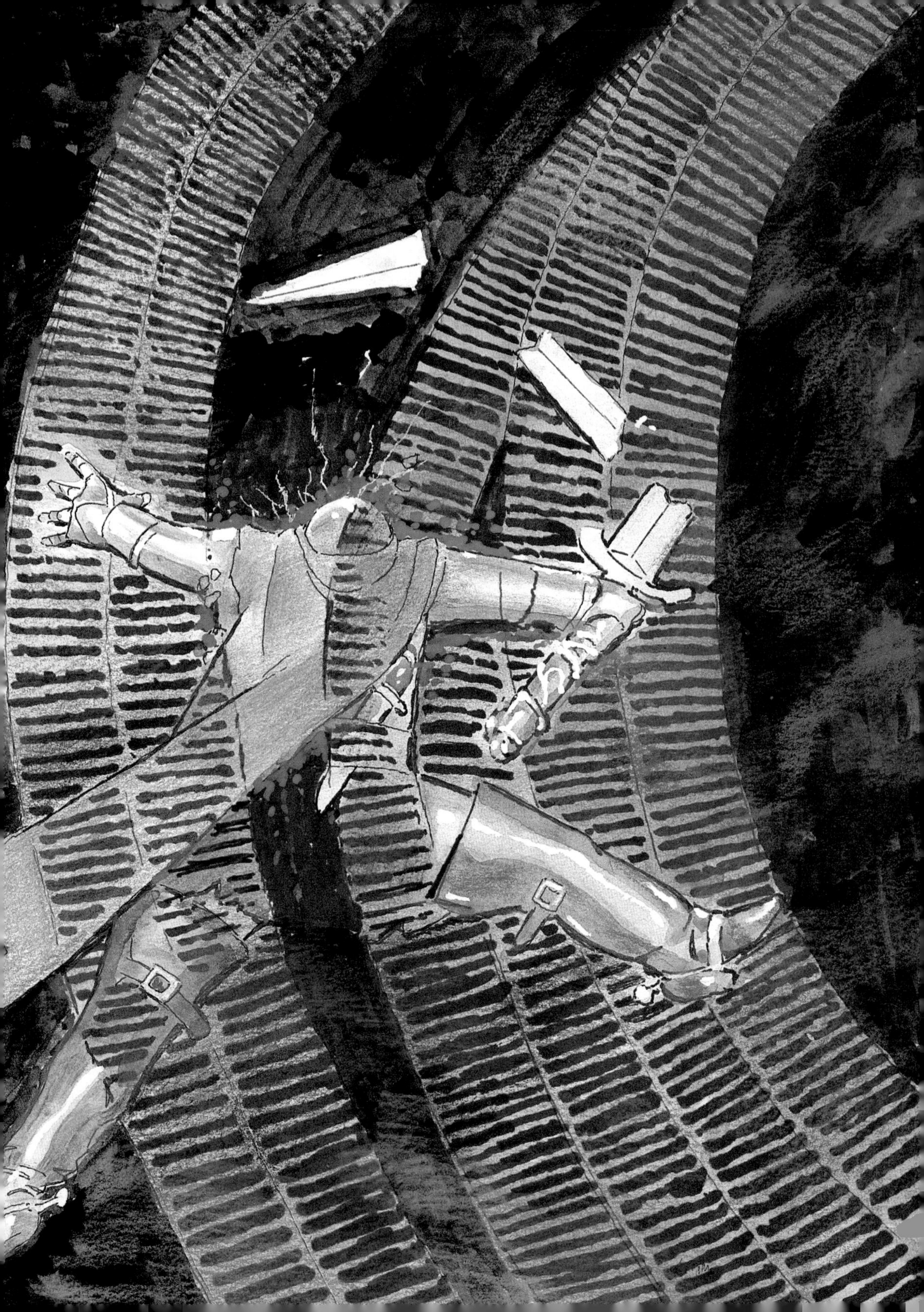

he last to know of the road were the Little People of The Shyer.* They had been forewarned by travelers passing through, but of course didn't believe in such stories, thinking them to be the wild imaginings of "outsiders."** Even after the tarmac had settled, and the Little People had come out of shock, none were prepared for the greater evil the road would bear on its hard shoulders.

*The Shyer: An idyllic oasis of rural tranquillity inhabited by a race of inbred Little People. They don't do a lot, and seem to be semi-retired. They like to loaf and potter around the garden. The only product produced in the Shyer, mainly for personal use, but sometimes exported, is garden weed. The weed, smoked in pipes, brings about a pleasant euphoria and a general sense that all's well in the world.

**Outsiders. This usually refers to the touring bands and troubadours who are well received in the Shyer, such as The Roving Ring Singers, The Bonzo Baggins Big Band, and Cypress Hill.

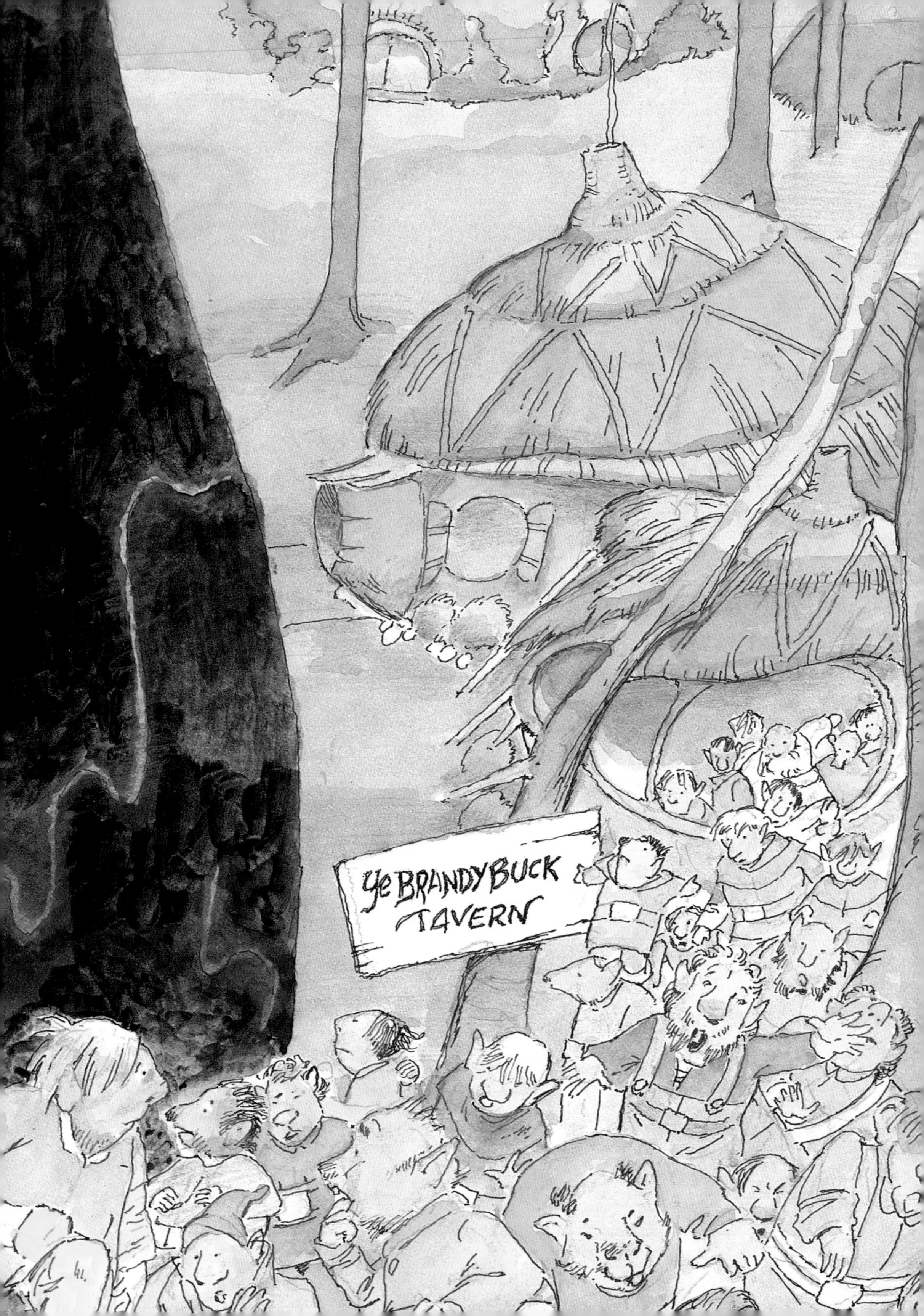
Ye BRANDYBUCK
TAVERN

n the Shyer, the Dark Rider had a field day. The Little People had not been so shaken since Old Mr. Brandytook planted his carrots in a circle instead of a line, or since Young Merryweather wore odd socks to the village fair. They were even more shocked than when big Mrs. Blaggins the blacksmith went psychotic and killed four of her family in the workshop, and each with a different tool. (Of course, she pleaded insanity and insisted the voices told her to do it . . . or, more particularly, Mr. Blaggins's voice, of which she had grown exceedingly weary.*

*This unfortunate incident, known as the Blacksmith Affair, is still widely talked about and discussed in Inns the length and breadth of the Shyer. Most are at a loss to explain why good natured Mrs. Blaggins went ga-ga and wiped out her entire family in one hot afternoon. Some, mainly the heavy users of brandy-skunk weed, claim that the whole thing was a conspiracy, and that some darker, all-powerful force was behind the killings. Yeah, right. As if. . . .

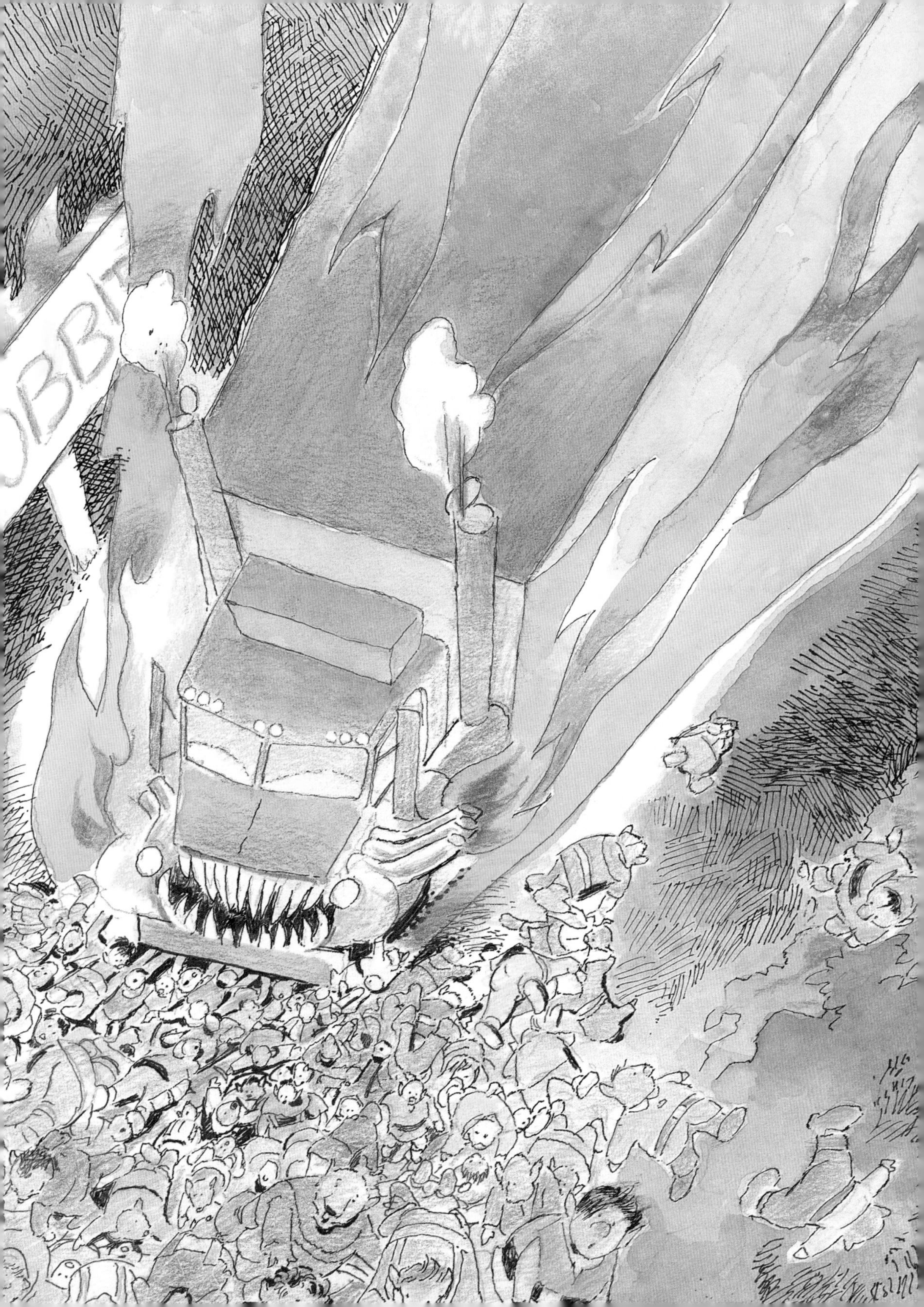

As the road came, some of the Little People ran and hid, only to watch in despair as their homes were subsumed by the ever-spreading tarmac. Others packed up all they owned and fled east toward the mountains.* For they feared Trolls much less than this new terror. Unfortunately, the road outran one famous family . . . but at least they got to put their newly bequeathed spoons to good use.

*Mountains. Among the Little People who fled to the mountains were a large contingent of brandy-skunk smokers. Seeing at first hand proof of the conspiracy of dark forces from outside the Shyer, they barricaded themselves into heavily fortified homesteads and formed themselves into Militias. Fearing what they called TOWO, The Old World Order, a conspiracy of Wizards, Trolls and Bankers, they became increasingly paranoid and isolated from their fellows, and took to taking potshots at anyone who turned up unannounced. This unfortunate behaviour resulted in the Brandy Ridge Incident, where one family mistook a Postman as an W.E.A.** Agent and dropped a twenty-ton rock on his head. This in turn ruined a card from their favourite Uncle inviting them over for a siege at his place, where they were all under attack from TOWO Trolls disguised as Postmen.

**W.E.A. Weed Enforcement Agency

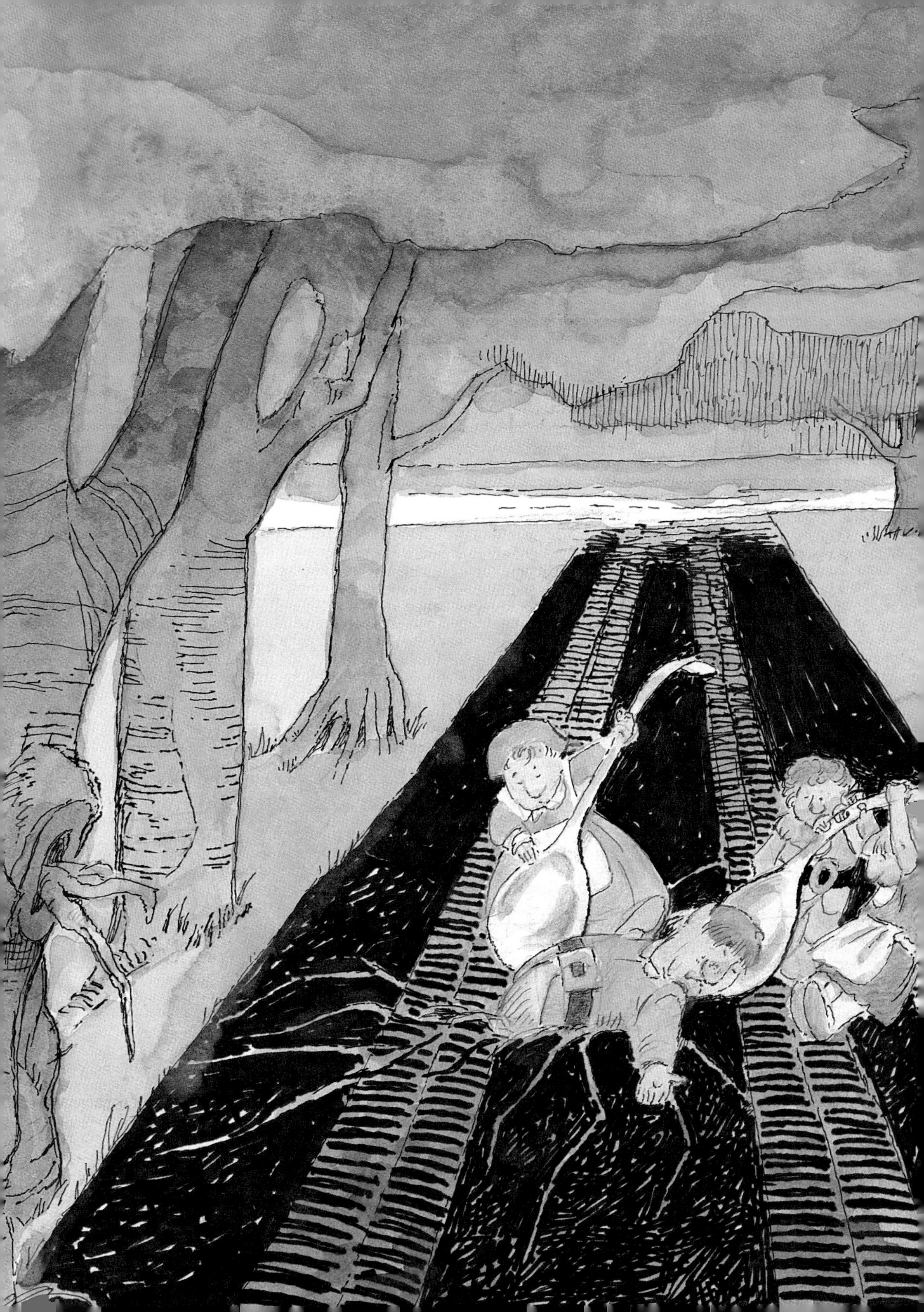

he Dark Rider was not the only terror the road brought to Middle Terra Firma. Along its pitch pathways deadly diners appeared. At first, none but the abominable fat, greasy creatures of the night (also referred to in some arcane circles as "truckers") paid them much heed. Then came the Trolls, wide-eyed burners of things at both ends. Finding the damp, roach-infested pit-stops to their liking, they butchered their owners and set up shop.*

*These massacres are told of at length in the Highway Ode and are often referred to as "The Horrible Things That Happened At The Diners Because of The Trolls."

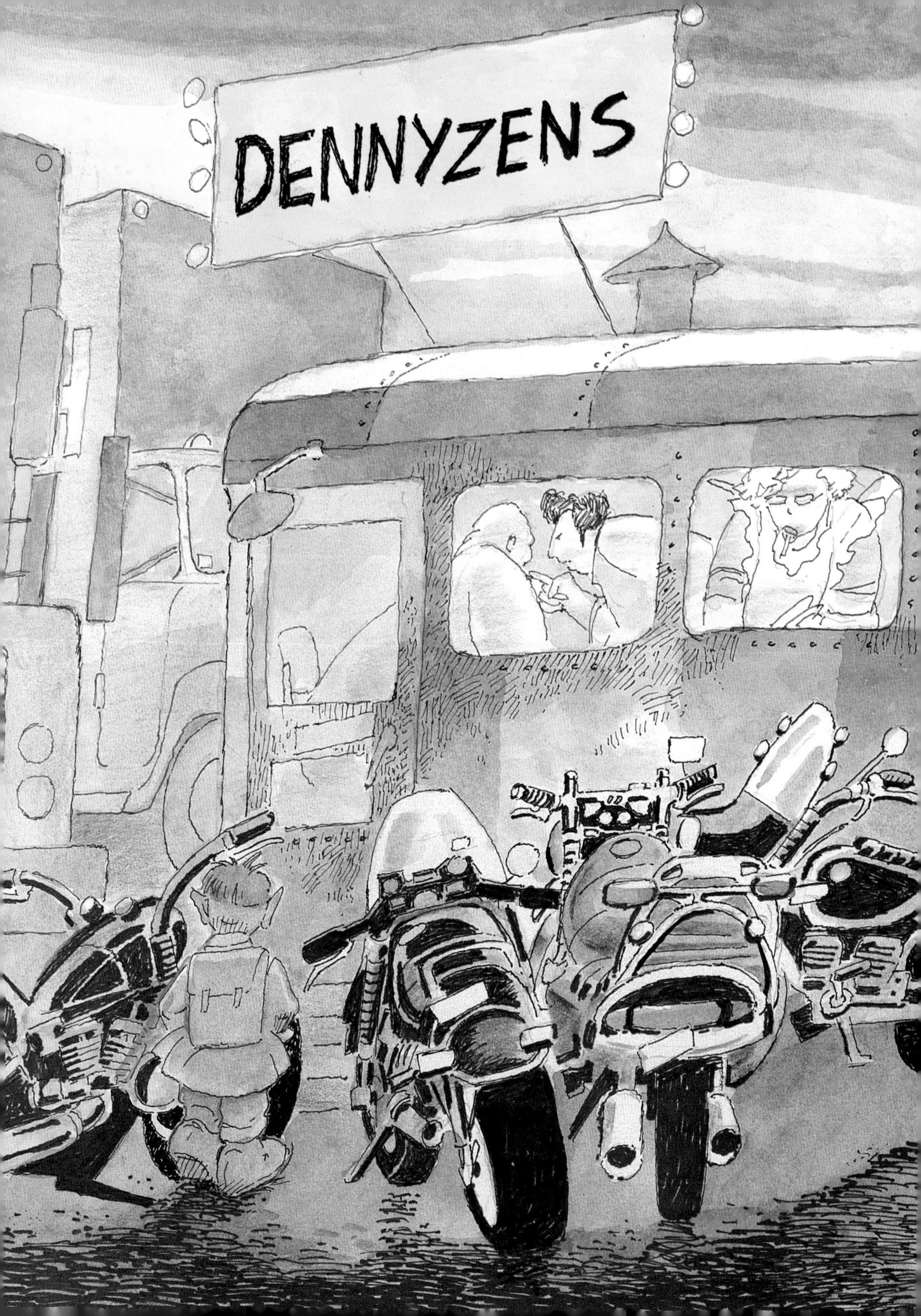
DENNYZENS

ome of the fleeing Halfwits from the Shyer found the promise of roadside fare at reasonable prices irresistible.* They sucked in their stomachs, stuck out their necks and stepped inside only to find the dish of the day a bit rare for their liking.

*Most diners offer a special "eat all you can" menu, very popular with those out for a late last supper. They're also very popular with the Troll waitresses who often get the tip that's left . . . as well as other unwanted body parts.

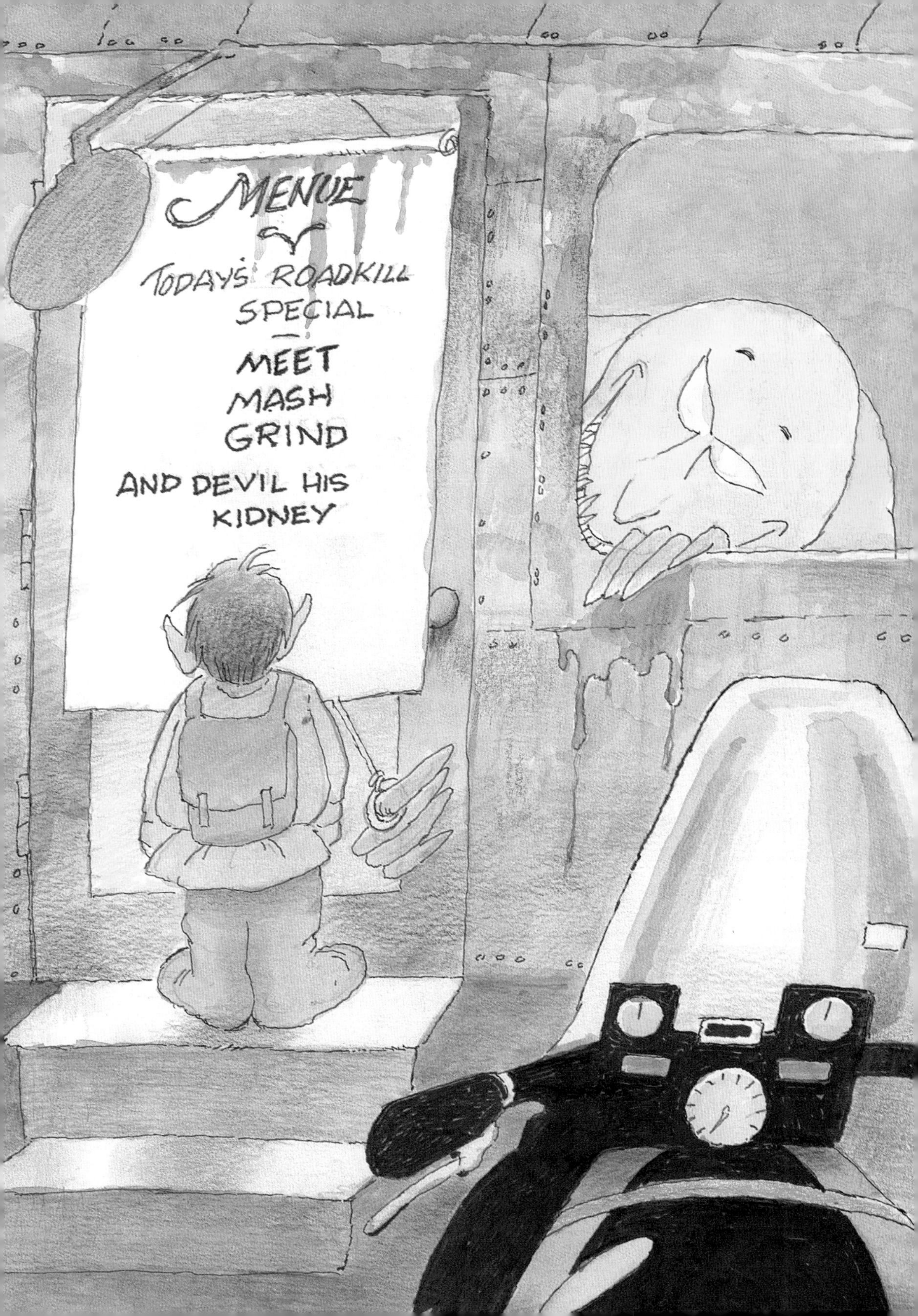
MENUE
TODAYS ROADKILL SPECIAL
—
MEET
MASH
GRIND
AND DEVIL HIS KIDNEY

he fava beans and chianti were in very bad taste, for they were far from specialties in the Shyer. In their haste to hie themselves away from the Dark Rider and forget for but a moment the terrors of the tarmac, the Little People also forgot the eating habits of Trolls. Brave Biker Trolls took the time to tenderize their meals, foolishly thinking they could later outrun the Dark Rider. They went from road hogs to roadkill before they had time to digest.

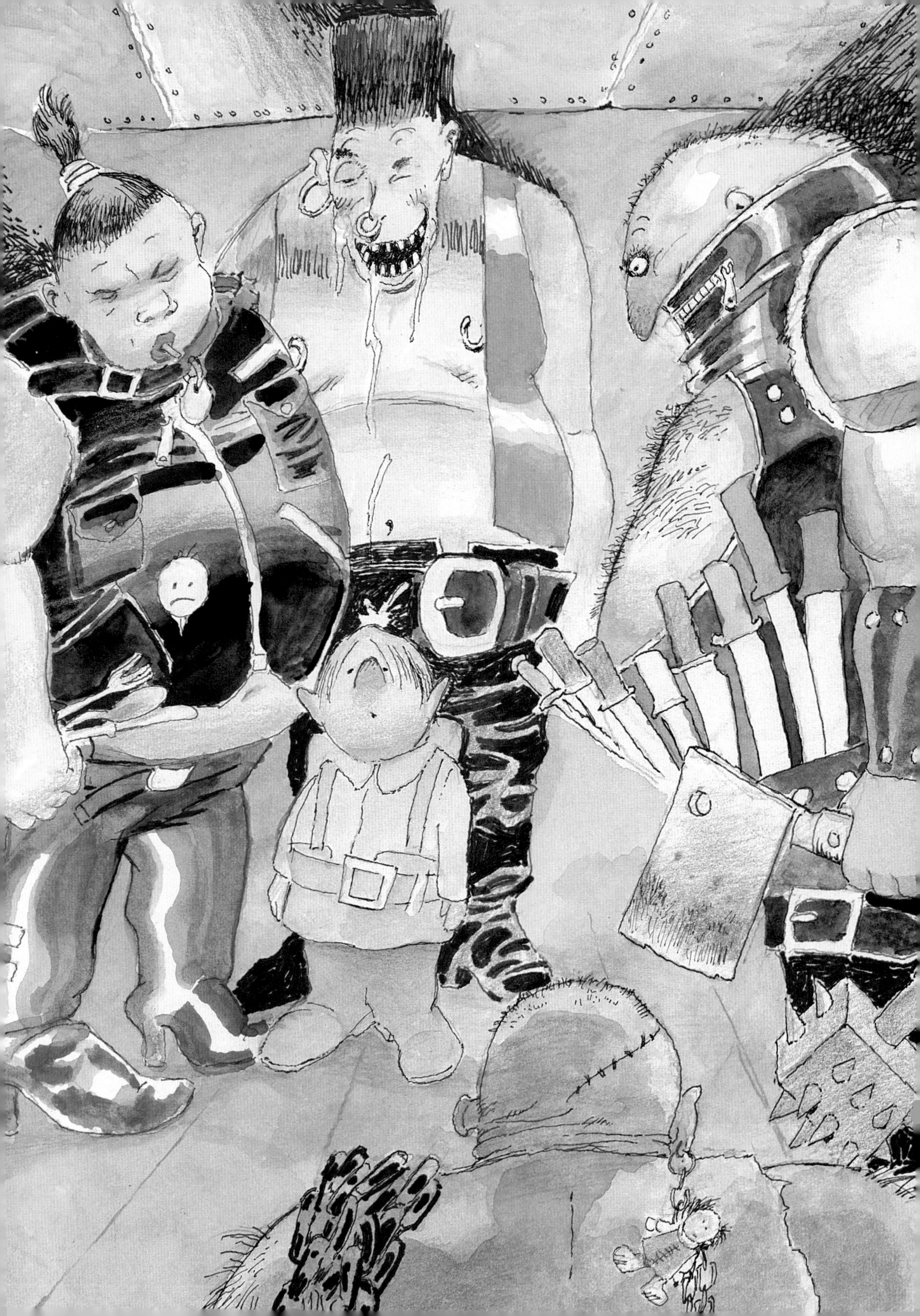

nd so it came to bypass that the road's snaking grip became vice-like. Slowly but surely its ebony coils began to constrict, choking the life out of Middle Terra Firma. All those of good intent and true heart who hadn't fallen by the wayside met for a great council in the timeless woods of Westlothian, the last stronghold of the old world. From the valiant and the titled to the lowliest Halfwit, they came. From the wisest Wizard to the dumbest Dwarf, a crusade was assembled to strike at the very heart of the darkness, the Tower of Tarmac-adoum, the stronghold of shadows.

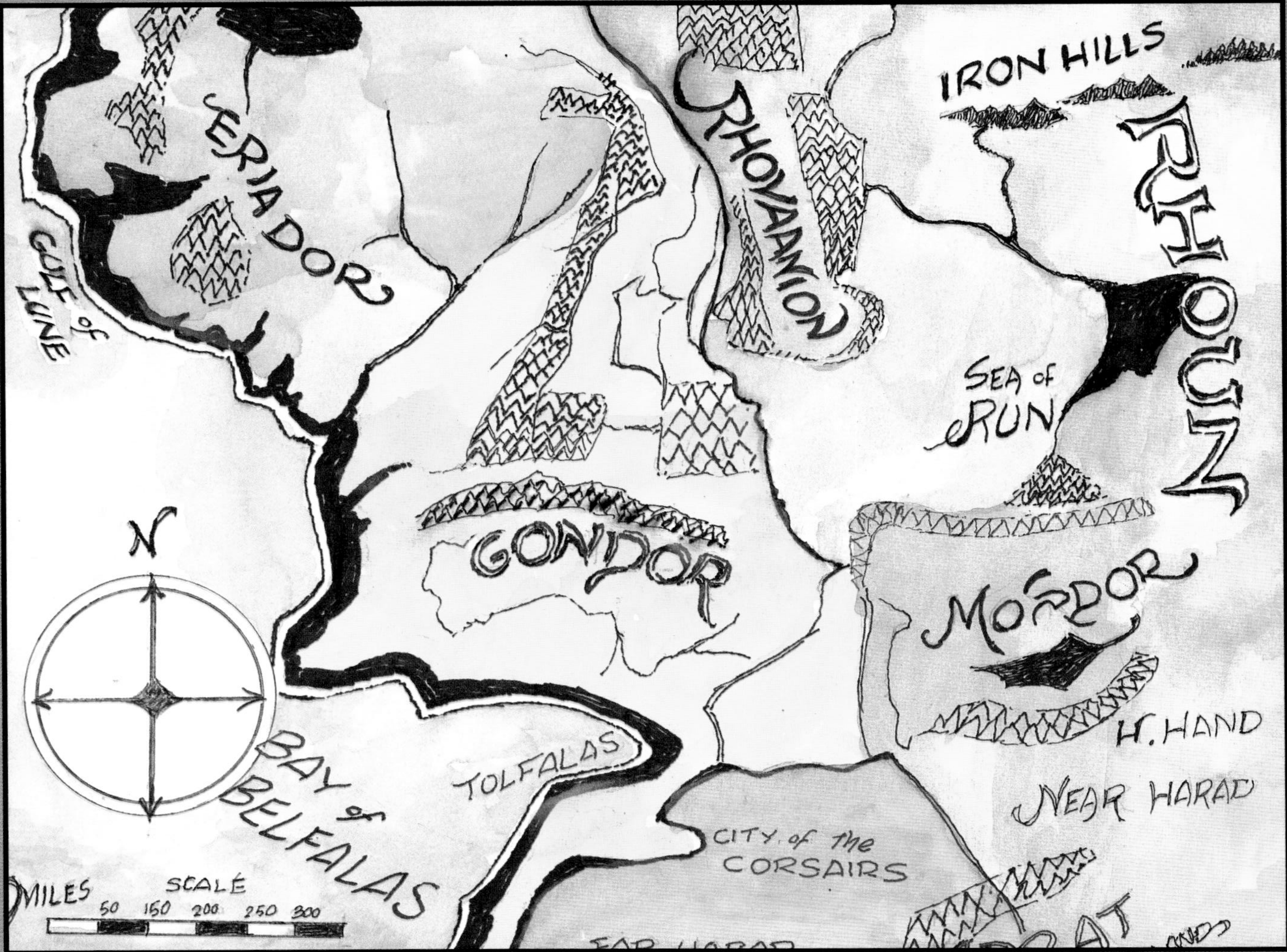
IRON HILLS
RHOUN
RHOVAANION
ERIADOR
GULF of LUNE
SEA of RUN
GONDOR
MORDOR
H. HAND
NEAR HARAD
CITY of the CORSAIRS
TOLFALAS
BAY of BELFALAS
N
MILES SCALE 50 150 200 250 300

armac-adoum, built on the ruins of the great multi-story parking garage of Enseepee, was said to be a catacomb of dark, dank spaces. Many an unsuspecting traveler had entered for a short stay, never to return. For in the labyrinth below lived a creature so foul that none could speak its name without rooning.* The Trolls spoke of it as "the master's pet." In Elven tongue it was known simply as "git."** Among all the Dark Lord's nightmarish creations, this was his most horrific. A spiteful, vindictive blood-sucker, with eight dark arms and twice as many eyes, a prolific hunter able to conceal itself in perfect stillness and then strike like lightning on its unsuspecting prey.

*Rooning: The act of vomiting, taken from the noun form "roon," which refers to the product of the act of vomiting.

**Git. A rough translation reads, Traffic Warden.

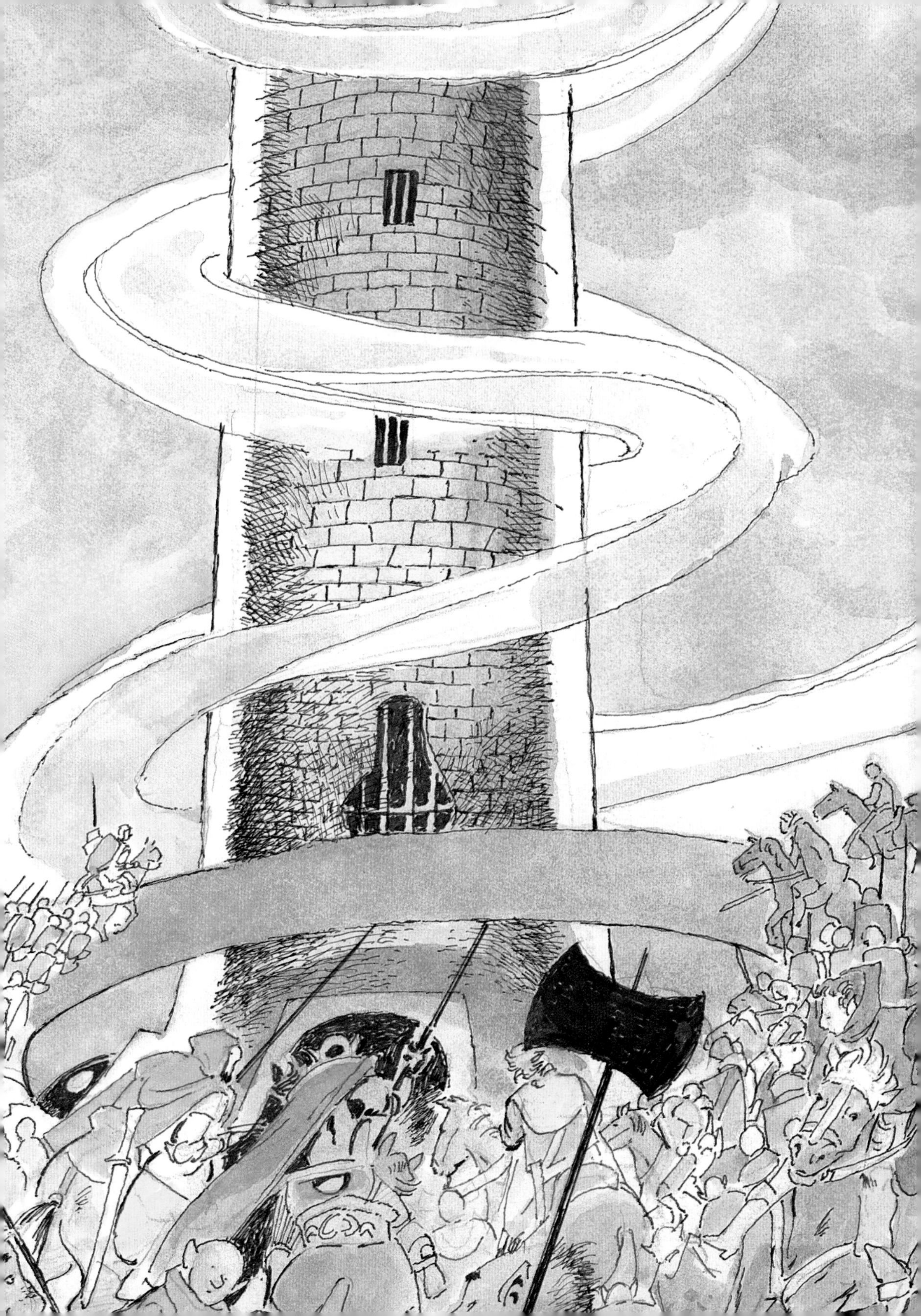

Wizard, a Dwarf, four Halfwits, a Prince, an Elf, and a Warrior were chosen. (In fact, many drew straws and they got the short ones.) Badly were they equipped, for there was a mighty shortage of useful things, like magic cloaks and broken swords, but they did not set out quite as naked as the evil one perceived.

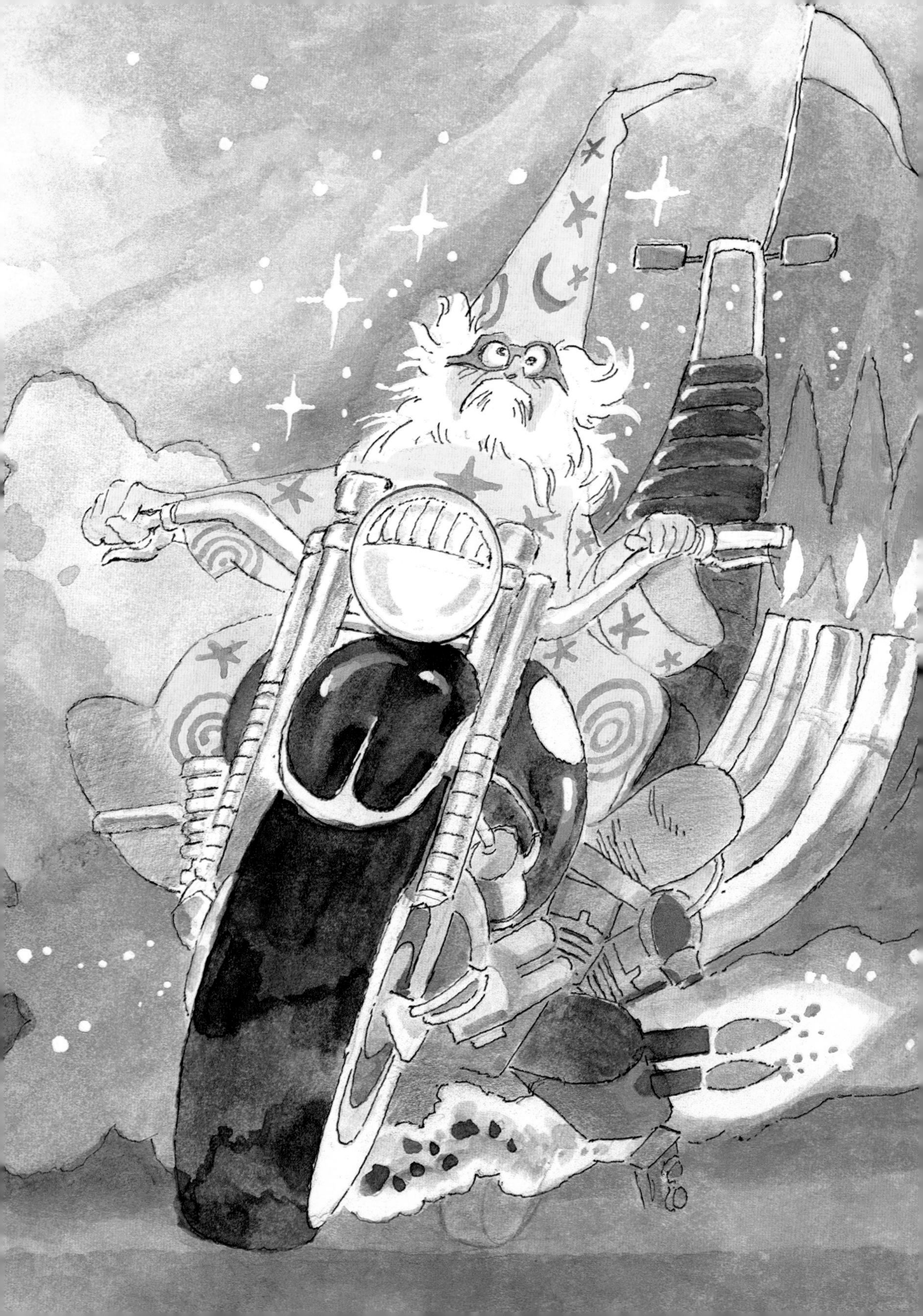

he Halfwits were presented with superbly crafted Israeli hand weapons and the finest body armour known to man or Elf. They were taught how to shoot indiscriminately at anything that moved, and how to justify their actions to the media using jargon such as *legitimate targets* and *collateral damage.**

*Collateral damage: An act of violence perpetrated on your unimportant second cousins or other direct line descendants not that well known to you.

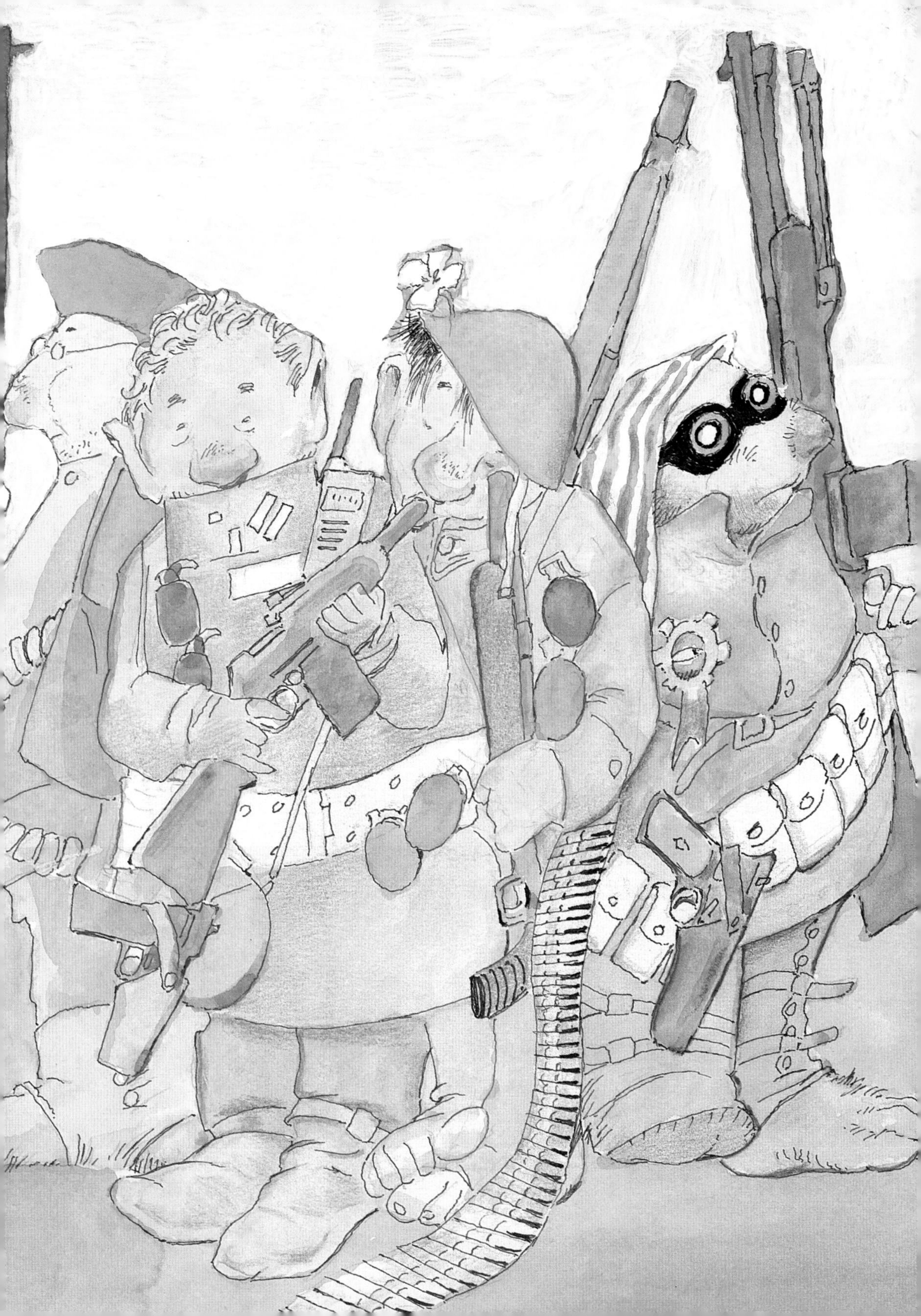

he Elf Legolando was gifted a trusty bow forged of steel by the Wildmen of Rambono.* Placid though he was at heart, some say the woods had put the zap on him and he should have been sent on a lengthy course of therapy before being given such a lethal weapon. (Others pointed out that using the weapon would allow for the release of pent-up aggression and was cheaper than therapy.)

*Wildmen of Rambono: Savage tribal Warlords who will never get to drive a fifty-seven Chevy until the tyres fall off, due mainly to two things. One, they live completely isolated in the jungle, and two, they'd probably attempt to eat anything that moved so slow and smelled so much of leather.

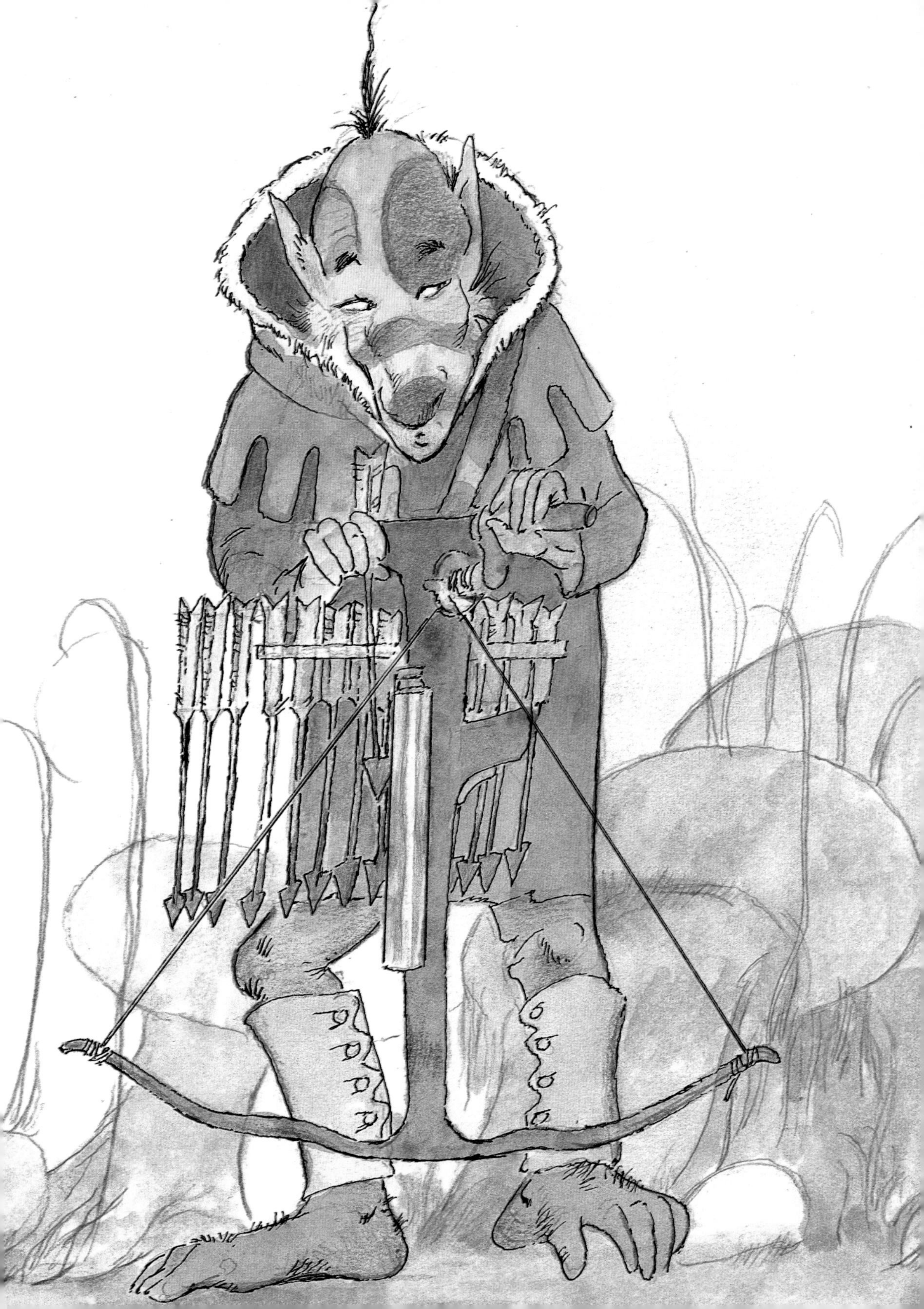

rince Garathorn, Defender of Crustini, Liberator of Jaydee, limped forth with a mighty sword* forged in the Firefights of Ram.** Years of battling the dark forces of Margate*** had definitely put the zap on him, but he was the only one who knew all the words to the battle tunes the Elves had crafted, and the only one prepared to sing their songs, even though it was in the rather ancient tongue of David Lee Roth.

*To the Prince, it was a sword. Others came to call it one as well, for those who did not come to taste its cruel steel (-jacketed projectiles).

**Firefights of Ram: Tribal battles, often to the death, fought out in the fight-pubs of highly violent seaside ports of the south coast of Winglund.

***Margate. Unruly seaport inhabited by strange, semi-evolved mutants. A collection of freaks banished from The Ram.

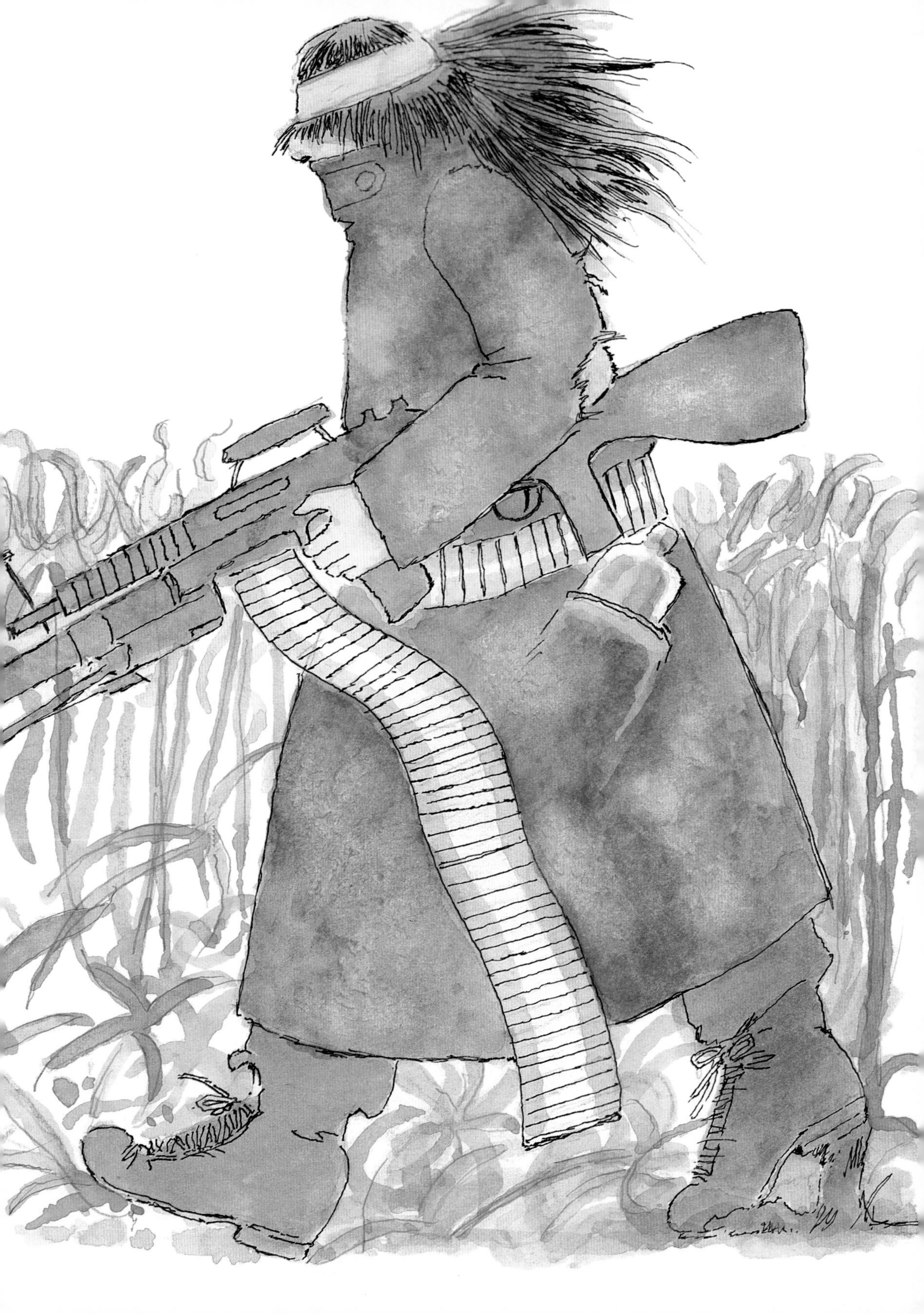

he Warrior, Borrownomore, wielded an axe bestowed upon him by the Wizard and Grandmaster of Illusion, Samrami.* Though fearsome a Warrior he was, the likes of whom had never been seen before, those with foresight and good taste in shlock horror knew that his fate was to be "dead by dawn."

*Samrami: Ancient and highly revered wizard of low-budget magic, used mainly in the defeat of evildead people. Thought to be deceased by some, a core following of disciples eagerly awaits his return and the bloodfest that will follow.

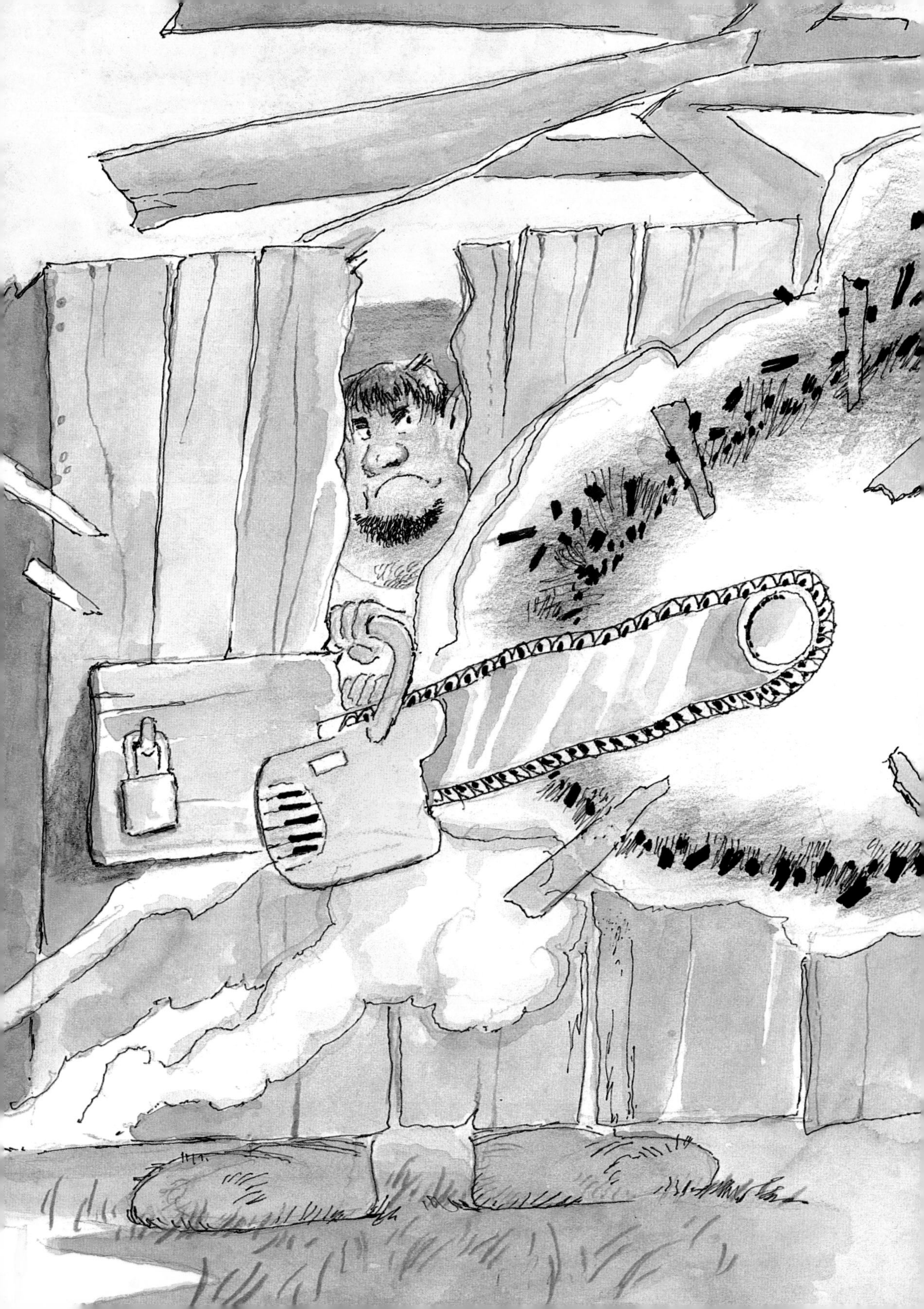

nd lastly, and by no means least, save his diminutive stature, Grimly, Son of Oi, brother to Loin, Gleen, Spleen and Mean, Grumpy, Bashful, Dozy, Dee, Mike and Titch, was presented with the Staff of Bazooka Joe (with which came free some x-ray specs and a rather fetching, if somewhat unconvincing, secret agent's beard).

*Bazooka Joe. Save and collect wrappers from their numerous candy products and receive free—excluding package and postage—any number of thrilling products. Save ten and you can apply for a toothless comb. One hundred gets you a DIY lobotomy kit. One thousand, a home assembly conspiracy-sniffer system. Ten thousand buys false teeth (with free overbite), to replace your own candy-rotted set. And, ultimately, one million wrappers gets you the Staff of Bazooka Joe—to be used only in times of national emergencies or if your home assembly conspiracy-sniffer system goes to code red.

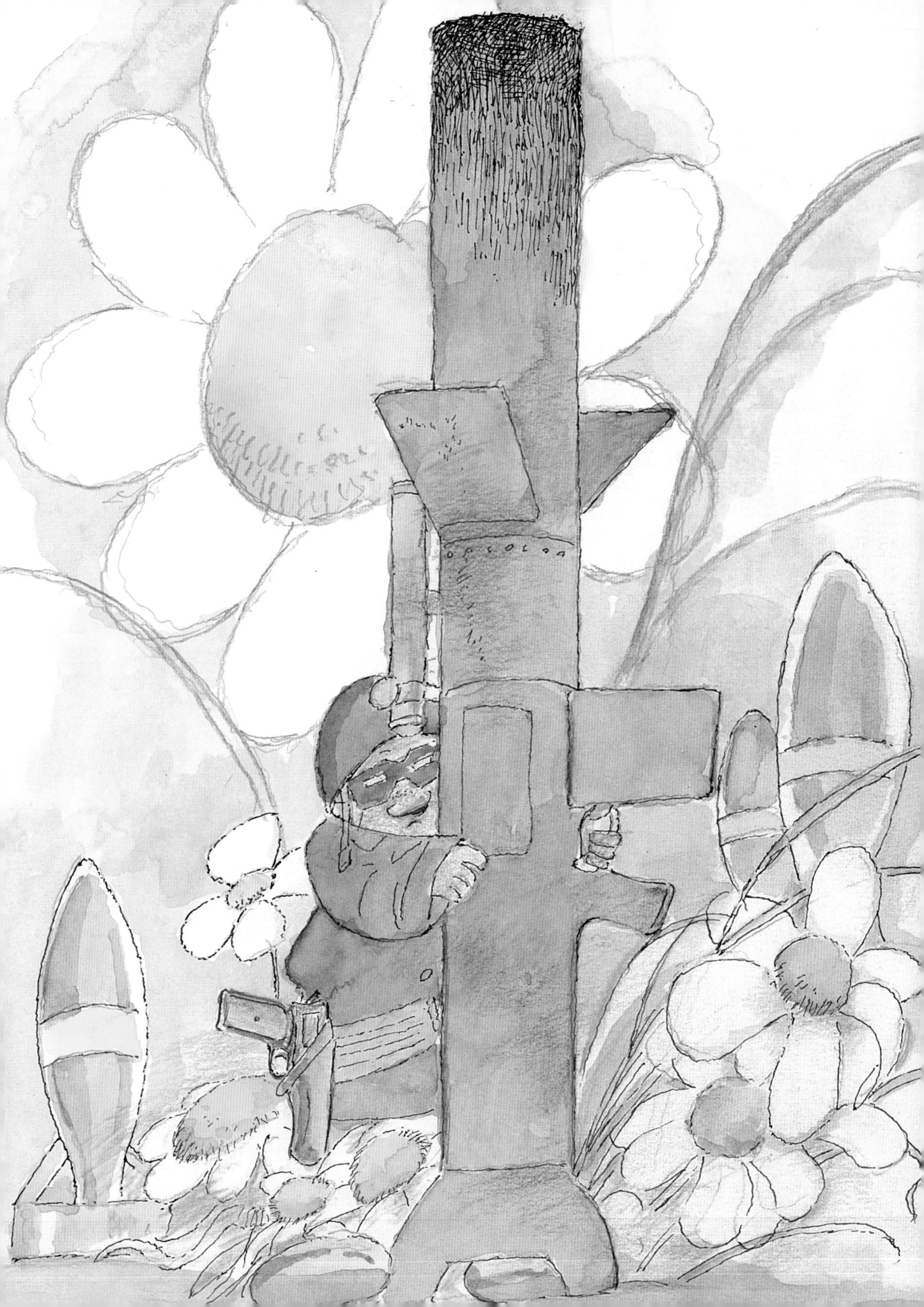

erily the final conflict began. The plan, to move by stealth across the hostile highways to within striking distance of the tower of Tarmac-adoum. But the enemy was ever watchful and by some unfathomable power knew of their coming.*

*The Dark Lord, being a Seer, had many mystical powers, one of which was not the power of Fung Shooey. His Tower was just so facing the wrong way. Doors opened onto stairs. Stairs led to blank walls. A downstairs toilet with the seat left up—and a torture pit laid with carpet instead of flagstones. No wonder there was so much bad energy about the place!

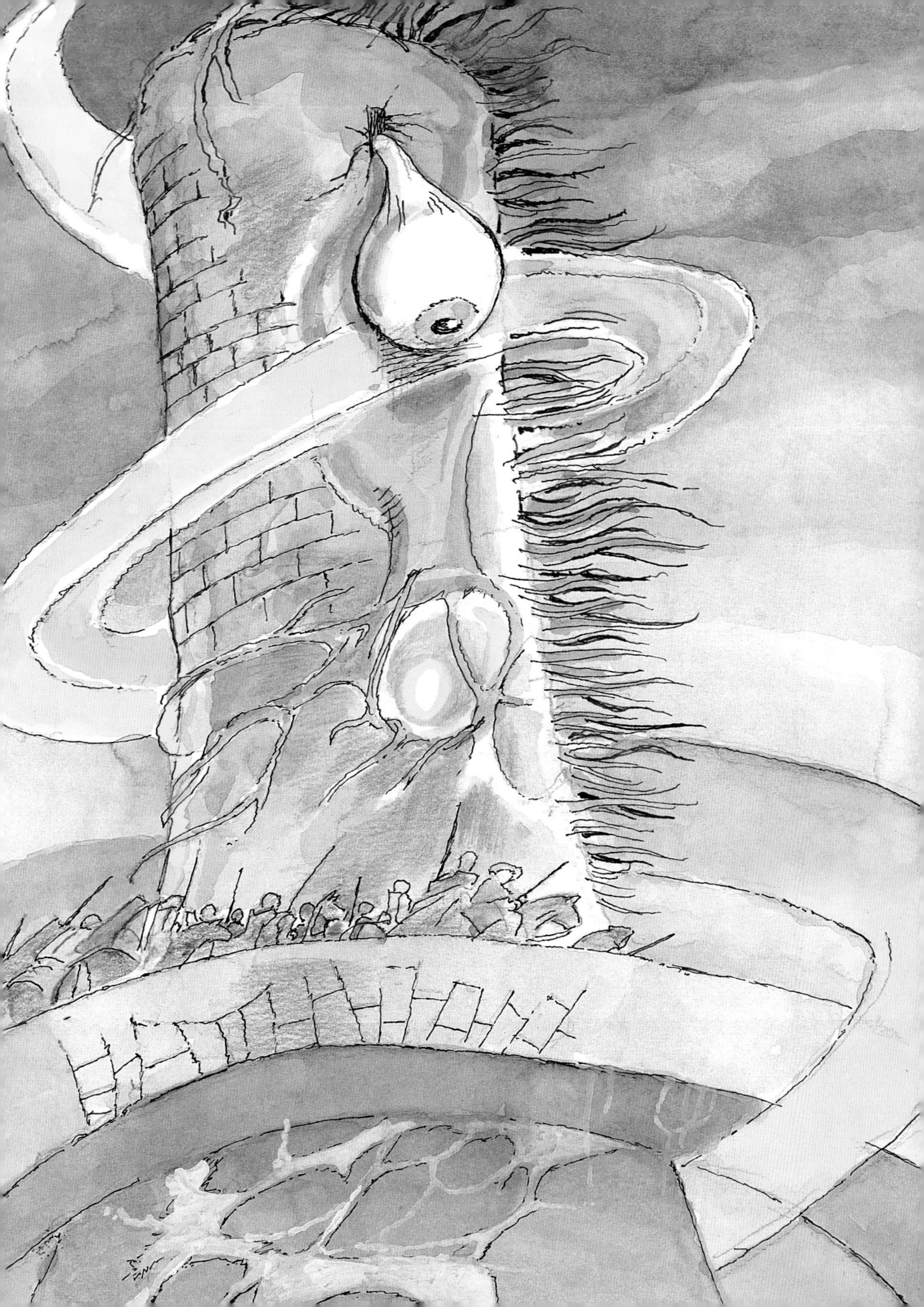

ithout warning a great automotive attack was unleashed upon The Best from The West. Lead by the Dark Rider, the horn-honking host swarmed down from dank parking lots under Tarmac-adoum. Borrownomore was the first to fall, cut in two by a Wraith that came out of the Sun. (See: dead by dawn.)

Legoland, in the face of overwhelming opposition, dropped his bow and surrendered . . . to his suicidal tendencies, and charged headlong into a pickup.

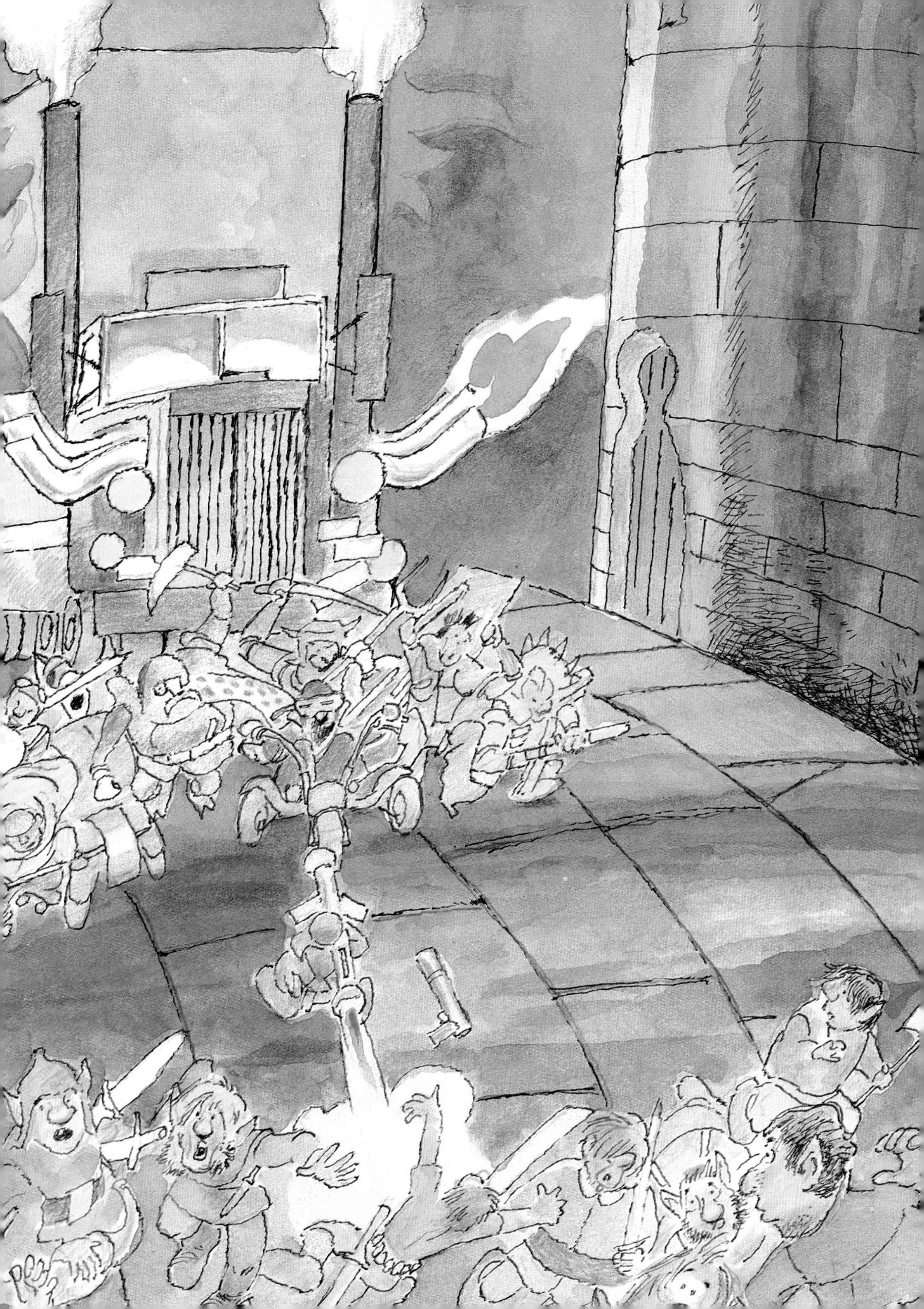

he Halfwits who, let's face it, were always on a one-way ticket to Palookaville, hijacked a bus and then blew themselves to bits.

The old Wizard, sensing things were not going their way, did a disappearing act, and finally, Prince Garathorn, brave and valiant to the last though he was, could not withstand the immense pressure bearing down on his royal personage and re-tyred . . . and The Best, as they say, were history.

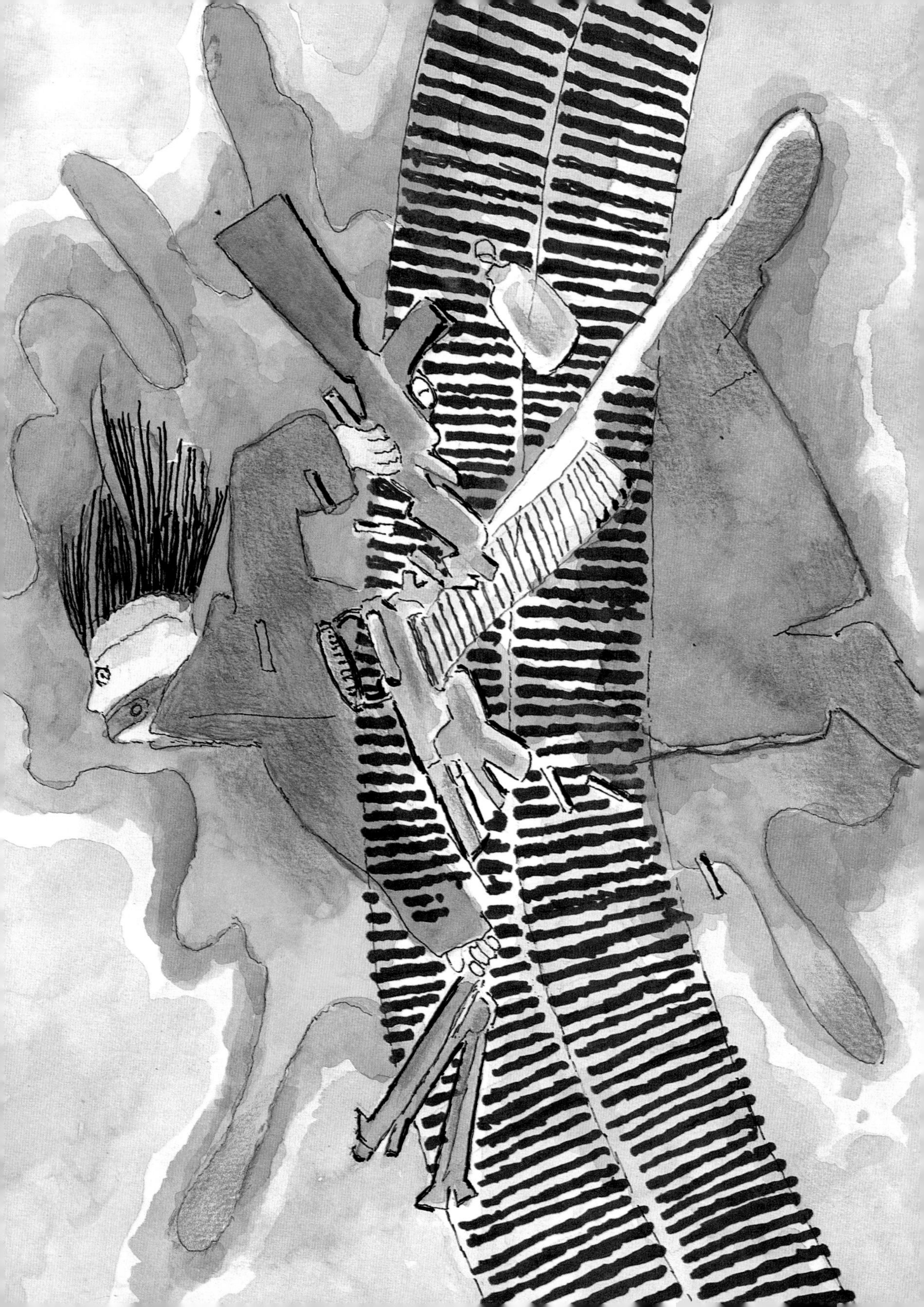

ith his enemy utterly van-squished, the Master of the Tower was free to step forth unhindered. Much was his surprise and glee to find the very thing that had eluded him all these years, embedded in some lowly roadkill. At last he had the means within his grasp to "bind all in shadow."*

*"Bind all in shadow:" Lawyer speake, meaning to tie people up in litigation so tight that they think they're back in Madam Spankbottom's dungeon.

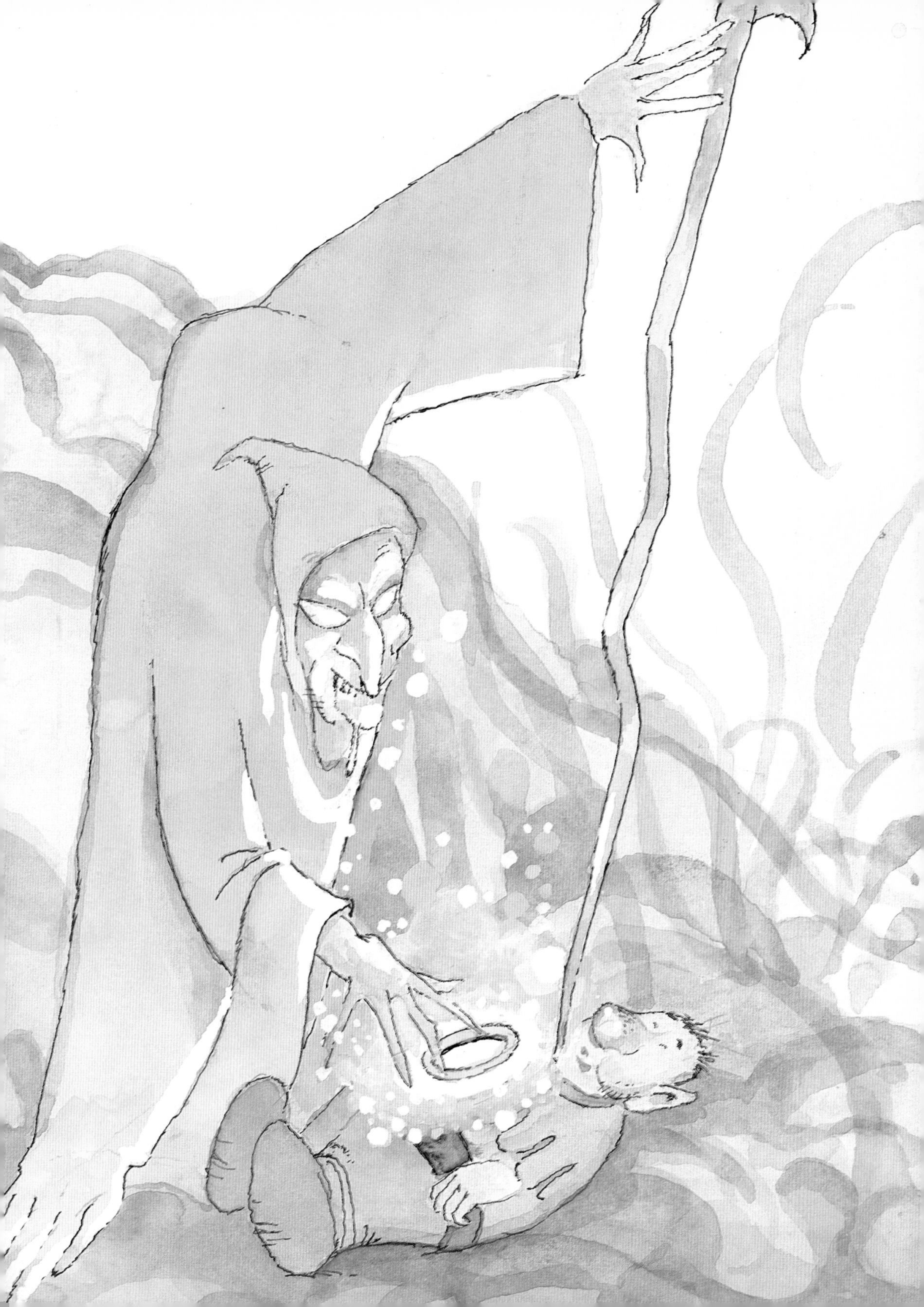

ut, the forces The Dark Lord had unleashed were selfish and would be slaves to none but their transport, and the (fluctuating with market vagaries) price of the blackest crude. A strange rhyme and unreason was upon them.* They could not be bound. Their vehicles he could not impound.

The Lord of Shadows should have learnt his highway code . . . and paid more attention when crossing the road.

*The scribe can no more fight this curse and ends it all in rhyming verse.

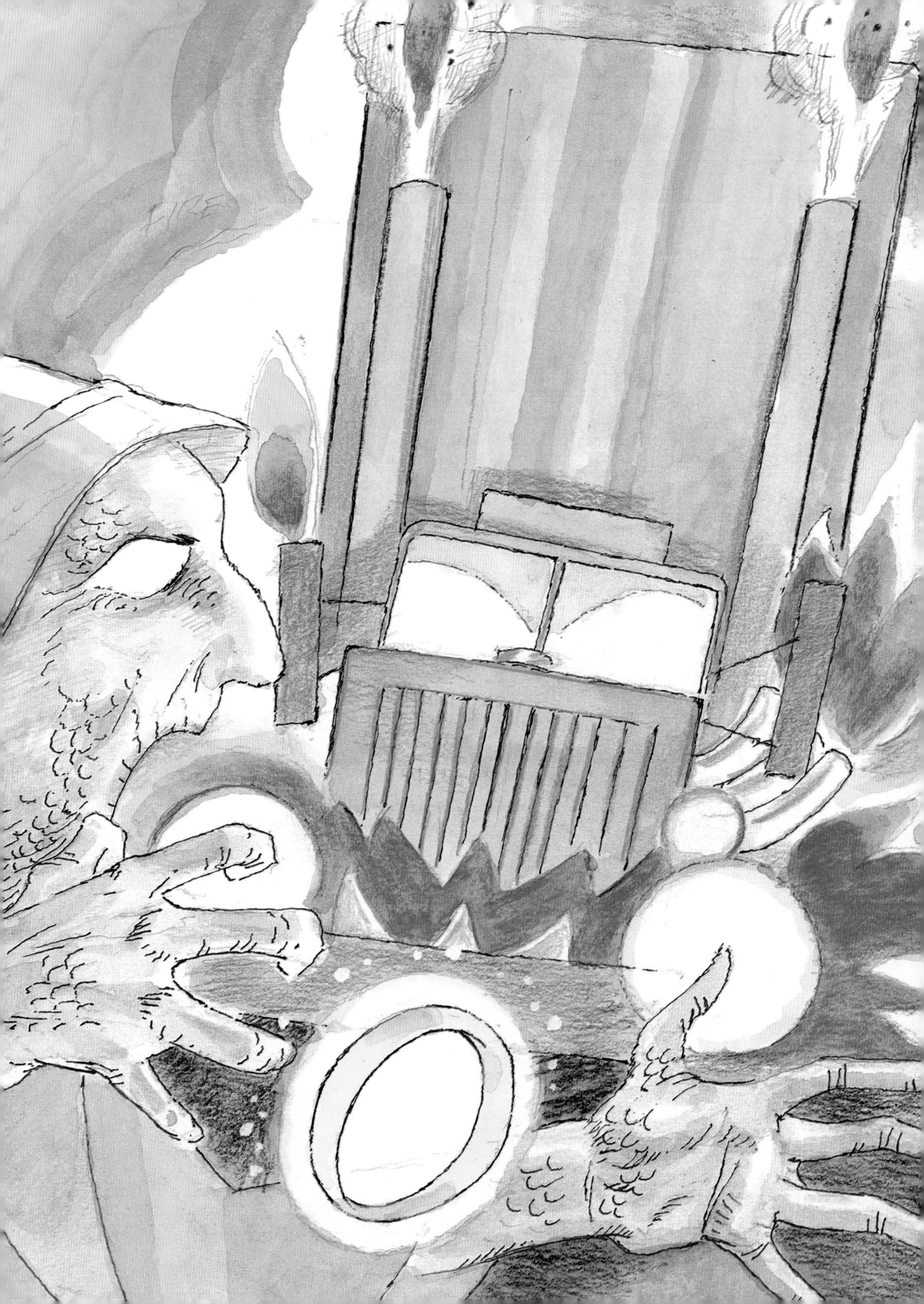

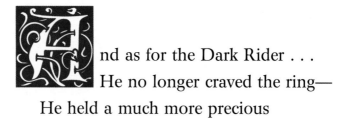nd as for the Dark Rider . . .
He no longer craved the ring—
He held a much more precious
    thing.
A ride to bear all through the night
the ramble of his musings trite.

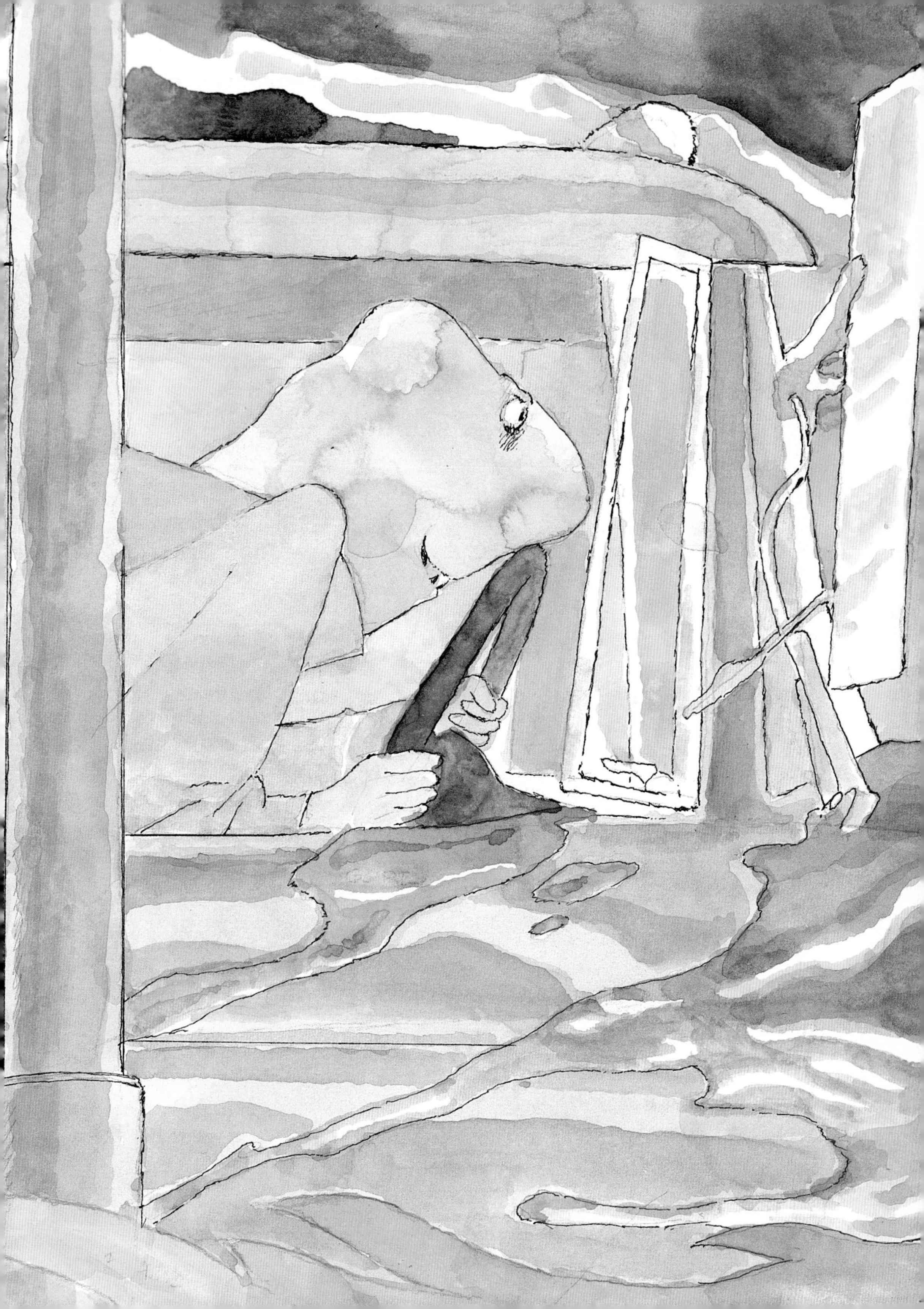

s talk and waffle were his whim
bad driving was the death of
       him.
How sad to see a sapling fall
Before the oldest of them all.

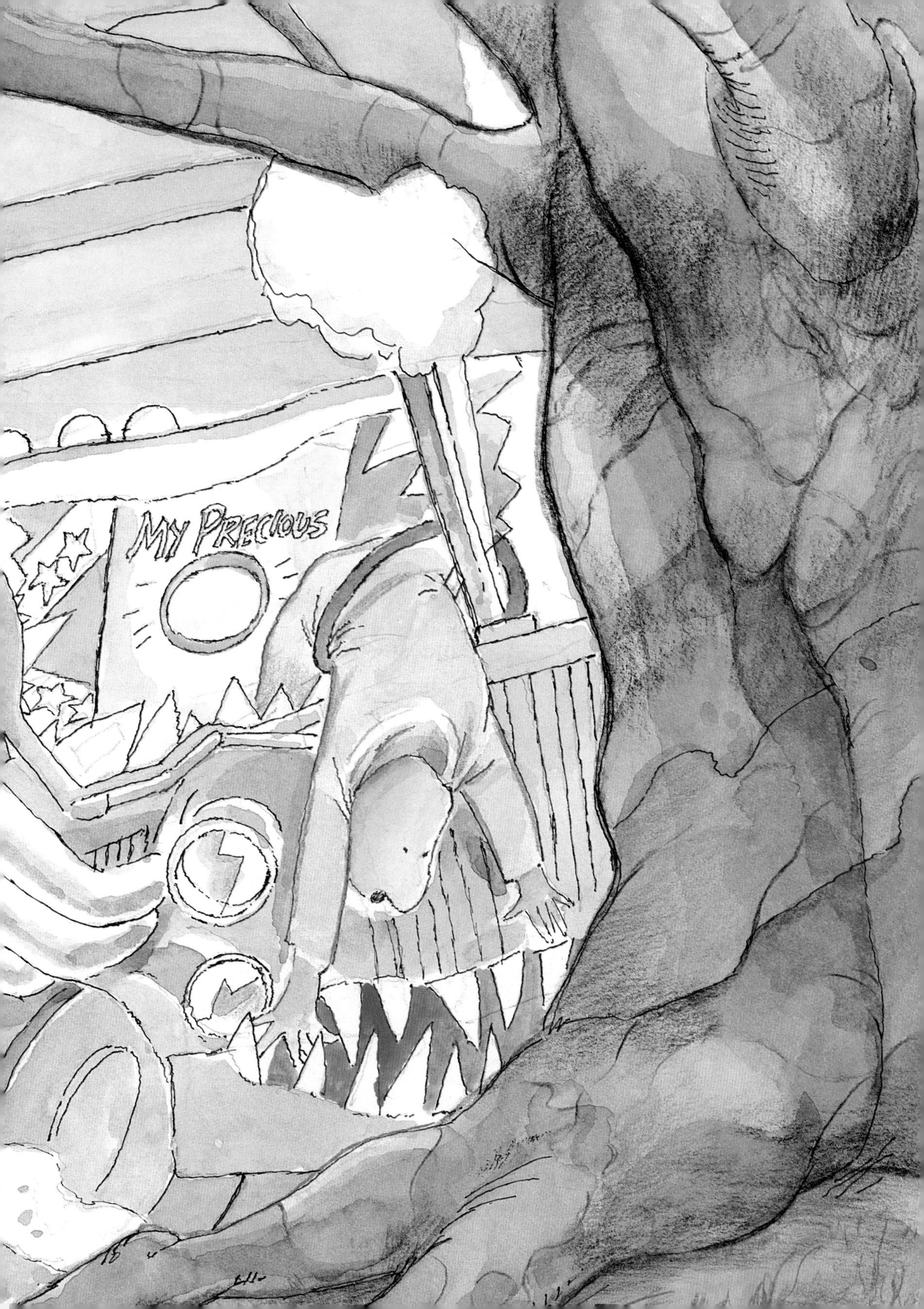
MY PRECIOUS

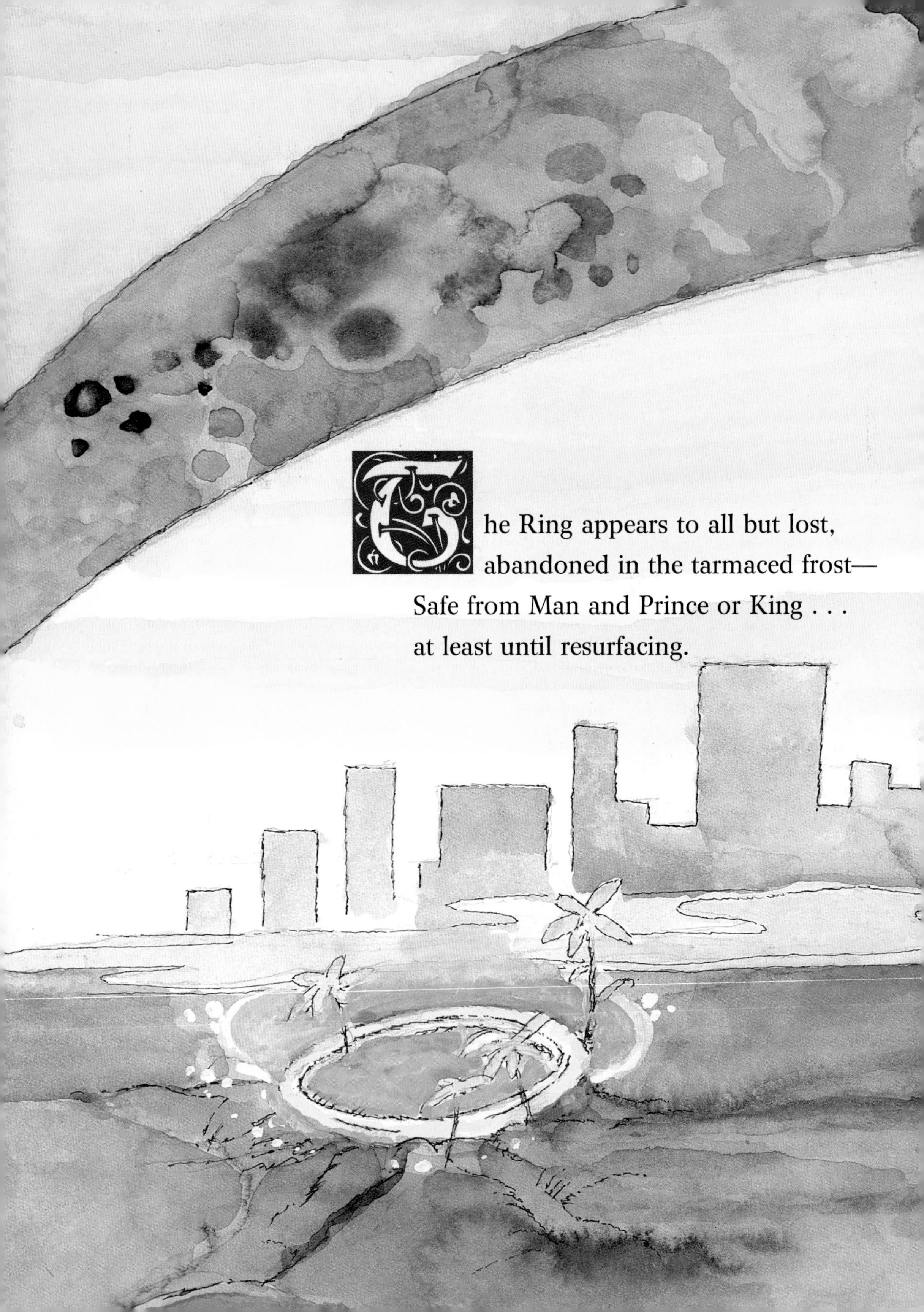

The Ring appears to all but lost,
abandoned in the tarmaced frost—
Safe from Man and Prince or King . . .
at least until resurfacing.